T0354865

SETTLED
Somewhere

GERALD WOLFE

WESTBOW
PRESS®
A DIVISION OF THOMAS NELSON
& ZONDERVAN

This is a work of fiction. All of the characters, names, incidents, organizations, and dialogue in this novel are either the products of the author's imagination or are used fictitiously.

WestBow Press books may be ordered through booksellers or by contacting:

WestBow Press
A Division of Thomas Nelson & Zondervan
1663 Liberty Drive
Bloomington, IN 47403
www.westbowpress.com
844-714-3454

ISBN: 978-1-6642-8656-6 (sc)
ISBN: 978-1-6642-8658-0 (hc)
ISBN: 978-1-6642-8657-3 (e)

Library of Congress Control Number: 2022922906

Print information available on the last page.

WestBow Press rev. date: 01/06/2023

CHAPTER 1

Somewhere Valley was changing. The people were the same, and they cared for each other just as much and helped each other every chance they had, but something was different about the way it felt in Somewhere Valley. Electric service had been extended to all the families living along the country road. New houses had been built, and Somewhere Chapel was planned on the hill in Somewhere Valley. A cell phone tower was visible on one of the hills near the Bar J Ranch.

Terry and Sarah Lund had built their home on a beautiful piece of land they'd purchased from the Bar J along the county road. Golden Girl, Sarah's new horse, had come to keep Traveler company in their new barn; and Shadow, a rescued military guard dog, reigned as the sentinel of the Rocking ST Ranch.

Terry woke early one morning before the sun had even begun to change the night into day. As he went into the great room of their home, he sensed something unusual. He moved toward the window to see outside but couldn't see anything. As he turned to go, he saw Shadow crouched at the door, one paw raised in alert as if he were about to spring into action.

Terry heard no sound coming from outside. He sensed something unexpected and hesitated, trying to decide what would be the best action to take for what unexpected event was about to happen. He slowly approached the door and cautiously peeked out the narrow window to see whether he could locate the source of his apprehension and Shadow's unusual behavior.

Sitting on the porch, leaning against the railing, was a man—at least it looked like a man—slumped over and apparently asleep. Terry reached for his revolver hanging on the coatrack beside the door and slowly turned the doorknob. As the door began to open, Shadow became more and more anxious to go out.

As soon as the door opened wide enough, the big shepherd dog bolted to the sleeping man on the deck and began barking. The man looked up and drew the dog into his arms as Terry stood, alert and confused. He came out onto the porch and realized who it was who had been sleeping there.

Tex was now wide awake and greeted Terry as he held the dog in his arms. Terry ran to join in on the greeting and sat down on the rough floor of the porch.

"How long have you been here?" Terry asked.

"Only a couple of hours. I decided it was too early to wake you and too late to get a bed inside, so I just went into survival mode and made myself comfortable here on this beautiful porch."

"I couldn't imagine why Shadow wasn't making more of a fuss over the stranger I saw on the porch. But you don't have to stay out here any longer. There will soon be some coffee in the pot, and I am sure Sarah will be glad to have you for breakfast. Come on in," Terry said.

As they came in, Sarah ran toward the front door, which had been left open. When she saw Tex, she engulfed him in a welcome hug and told him to put his things in the last room on the right while she fixed some breakfast and made fresh coffee.

"What brings you here, Tex?" Sarah later asked at the breakfast table.

"My protection agency has assigned me to be here for a few months since there has been some indication that there may be some activity here again. I thought about the first time I was assigned to place surveillance equipment around your place when Sarah was in such danger from the cartel. The memories and our friendship made accepting this assignment easy. It has been quiet for quite a while, but recently movement and suspicious events have put you and Sarah on the radar again. I'm not sure just what kind of situation exists, but here I am. I understand that another agent will be along in the next week or so. We are to try to wrap up the loose ends on this assignment so it can be put in the history books as a successful campaign," Tex said softly. "I was surprised by the yard light that came on when I started into the aspen break. It was a welcome surprise. Have you had any problems lately?"

"Everything has been so quiet," Terry said. "We were becoming a little careless. A couple of things that happened made us more vigilant but nothing big. Sarah and I began riding our horses to Carl's so they would get some exercise, since it is only about a mile to his gate and a short trip down his winding lane. We saw a suspicious-looking car one morning, and it passed us on the way home again that night, so we started carrying our guns in the saddlebags, but there's been nothing since. Our artillery is still in the saddlebags, since we haven't had a reason to use them, and we are thankful."

"That is good news. You don't want to challenge someone who has more experience with a gun than you do. My protection agency doesn't have anything specific, but we have heard some rumblings from other sources. I am glad I could be the one assigned. Both of you are a real part of my life as well as the rest of the Somewhere Valley folks. So you finally put Golden Girl in the barn?" Tex said, laughing.

"I did," Sarah said. "Carl was right. That pony was stubborn, but the challenge just made me love her more. I don't think she would hesitate to defend me or let me ride her anyway, anytime now."

"How often do you go with Terry when he is at the Wilsons'?" Tex asked.

"We go together all the time," Terry said. "We built a new training arena, and Sarah is training owners to treat their horses as valuable friends, not slaves. Carl couldn't be happier, and business is really booming, so having Sarah on the team is a real asset."

"It sounds like you are a lot happier too," Tex said.

"Couldn't be better," Terry and Sarah answered together and laughed.

The conversation covered all the details since Tex had been there almost two years earlier. The change in Somewhere Valley was amazing since electricity had been provided. Tex wondered whether they had phones now and found out that the tower really was what he thought it was.

"I want to rest most of today and make plans for the next month," Tex said. "I need to check in and let my boss know how things look. I want to go with you to Wilsons' and maybe even look for a horse I could ride while I am here. I don't suppose you would mind a border in your barn when I leave, would you?" He laughed.

CHAPTER 2

Sarah and Terry rode into the Wilsons' yard, but something didn't seem right, and they felt that danger was very near, so they changed course and rode behind the barn and left the horses there. They took their pistols and went around to the other side of the barn, approaching the back door of the house.

Terry went up the porch stairs and crouched low to get to the door. He felt there was no time to lose but wasn't sure just what to do. He motioned to Sarah to go to the front door and knock loudly. When he heard the knock and Sarah calling, he tried the back door, which was unlocked, and slipped in quietly behind a man with a gun, who stood in the doorway to the dining room.

Terry moved quickly and hit the man with his pistol, knocking him to the floor. The man's gun went sliding toward Carl. Terry saw Carl pick up the pistol and called to Sarah to come on in. Sarah entered cautiously and saw the man on the floor and Terry tying his hands together with his own belt. She ran to Carol, who was standing in the hallway, shaking like a leaf, and threw her arms around her to comfort her.

"What was going on?" Terry asked.

Carl sat down, still shaking from the encounter. "Frank was sure I had given him a bad deal on a horse and was going to make sure I couldn't cheat anyone else. He was so angry. I couldn't reason with him, and then he pulled the gun on us. I thought we were both goners until I heard Sarah call and knock on the front door. I figured you must be somewhere near, and I told God how thankful I was you were around, even if something terrible might happen. Thankfully it didn't."

He shook his head, looking at Terry. "But now what do we do with Frank? I thought he was a friend, but he sure didn't act as though he ever was, and it was such a simple problem to solve. He could have any two horses he wanted without this angry, dangerous outrage."

Frank groaned as he began to regain consciousness. He turned his head and saw Carl kneeling beside him. Tears came to Frank's eyes as he thought about what he had done.

"You are going to be all right," Carl said. "Terry came just in time to pull the fuse out of the dynamite. We can work something out, can't we?" Carl untied Frank's hands and helped him sit up.

"I don't know what happened to make me so …" Frank couldn't go on and just stared at the floor. "You must think I am awful!"

"We have known each other a long time. So let's just fix this problem between us and be friends," Carl said. "What would you like to do? You can take any two other horses you choose, and I will take the one back, even come and get her."

Frank just stared at Carl for the longest time.

Seeing that everything was safe now, Terry and Sarah slipped out and continued their work of training the two horses, which were to be picked up the next day.

When Carl came to the corral, Frank was driving out of the yard.

"I can't imagine why he got so angry," he said to Terry and Sarah. "He has never acted that way before. We have traded horses many times in the past, and he was never dissatisfied. But I think he is having trouble with one of his sons, and he and his wife are fighting about it."

He glanced at Sarah. "How are you coming with your horse, Sarah? I think the owners are coming tomorrow to pick him up. I hope you can pound some sense into their stubborn attitudes, but I wouldn't count on it."

The rest of the morning went smoothly, and Carl suggested they take the afternoon off. Sarah and Terry rode slowly out of the yard toward home. Out on the county road, they let the horses lope toward their property. The cold air seemed to clear out a lot of anxiety, and they looked forward to being home.

Meanwhile, after looking around the Lund home and checking for anything suspicious, Tex left to visit the other ranchers.

Late in the afternoon, he drove into the yard as Terry and Sarah were putting their horses in the barn. He went to the barn and asked how their morning had been. Sarah's account of the day's events made everyone feel better that it had ended as it did.

Terry asked about Tex's morning visits and found that he had gone only to two other places. Everyone wanted to spend time with him, so he didn't get everything done that he wanted to. But it was enough, and his ties of friendship grew in Somewhere Valley.

"When is this new agent supposed to arrive?" Sarah asked at supper.

"I don't know for sure, but I get the impression this week, maybe by Friday," Tex said.

On Friday morning, Tex's ringing phone startled him out of sleep. He answered sleepily but was wide awake when he heard the message. He was to pick up the agent in Cody on the last flight, at about seven thirty p.m. The agent would be staying with the Martins, and maybe he could take her there. Tex caught the "her" and wondered if it was Jill, who had been part of the original team protecting the Martins and Sarah. She had the best understanding of the whole situation from the beginning with Sarah and would be ideal in renewing her contacts there in Somewhere Valley.

At breakfast, Tex shared the news, and they all decided to go to Cody. Terry went to the Martins' place to ask whether he could use their pickup since it had a full back seat. When he told them what was about to happen, Molly Martin said she hoped Jill would be able to come back. Terry hadn't thought of who the agent might be, but having Jill back would be a real treat for Sarah.

Tex and Sarah were ready to go when Terry got home, so they left for Cody. Shadow was left outside to guard the house. The special doggy door into the barn would give her a warm place if the weather got too cold.

CHAPTER 3

When they arrived in Cody, Terry turned in at the second-hand store, where they had bought their wonderful dining table. They were looking for a single bed for Tex's room to replace the cot. They found just what they were looking for and loaded it up. Tex asked whether they could include in the load a table he had found. The shopkeeper was very helpful and easily loaded the table and six chairs.

"While we are in Cody," Sarah suggested, "we should buy groceries too." They would have more choices here. So they spent a long time in the supermarket. Tex bought some snacks for his backpack, and they left to eat lunch.

Just as they turned into the Broken Wheel parking lot, Rob and Lottie Evans turned in behind them. Rob had wanted to see Sarah and Terry since more information about Sarah's family became available. When she had been taken from them, she had still been a teen. Rob had become involved with Somewhere Valley folks shortly before Sarah showed up.

"I have word that something has happened to your father in Ohio," Rob said to Sarah after greeting them. "I don't know the exact circumstances, but it could be important. Do you know where any of your family might be, brothers or sister or mother?"

"I don't think anyone has heard from my brothers in years. I didn't know I had a sister, but it could just be one of the girls my mom took in from time to time to help them get a better start in the world. My mother wasn't well when I was abducted, so I am pretty sure she's no longer alive, and my father was probably off working like he always did, away from home."

"We are planning to go to Somewhere Valley this week sometime, so maybe we will have more information by then," Rob said.

Lunch was just as good as always. Of course, Tex had to listen to Rob tell the story of how they had met and how Molly got hurt with all the details. Lottie asked about the news from Somewhere Valley, and for once there weren't any terrifying situations to report. Finding out Tex had been assigned long-term was comforting, and that they had come to Cody to pick up another agent on the last flight was also good news.

Arriving at the airport just as it was getting dark, Terry didn't say anything but noticed Tex was somewhat nervous. Not rock-solid calm as usual. They exchanged knowing glances as they talked about old times. The plane landed just after seven p.m., so the trio went into the terminal. Tex was way ahead of Terry and Sarah.

"Why is he so nervous?" Sarah asked.

As they entered the terminal, Terry spotted Jill. "I think there is your answer, Sarah. We'll just have to wait and see."

Moving around a group of people, they saw Tex and Jill's meeting. Tex still seemed very nervous; he was talking loudly and moving around a lot.

"Do you have another bag?" Tex asked.

"Yes, that big brown and white one that just came in," Jill answered.

Since Tex and Jill had worked together in the early days, protecting Sarah from being harmed after the cartel discarded her, they had built a strong bond with each other. Neither was sure it had become more than that, but each hoped it would.

On the way home, questions and answers came from both Terry and Sarah, but Tex was unusually quiet most of the time. Jill wondered what was wrong as Terry told Jill about the troubles they had encountered and said that recent events had been pretty quiet.

"Thank God," Tex said softly.

Jill glanced his way, wondering whether something big had happened and became even more curious about his responses and Tex's actions. Neither knew how the other felt about their relationship, but both wanted more than they had seen so far. Jill struggled with Tex's faith and wondered whether there had been a change in his understanding of his relationship with God. The remark seemed to indicate that a change had taken place, and she welcomed the hope that had sprung up within her.

The rest of the drive home was mostly quiet. When they turned into the Martin ranch, Jill noticed the new house. Her questions and his answers were thrilling, and she quietly thanked God for His protection.

As they backed up to the back door and unloaded the furniture and groceries, Shadow's bark greeted them as he ran alongside the truck. All of them were tired and went to bed as soon as they were settled.

The sun was coming over the eastern ridge. Terry got up and put a log on the smoldering embers in the fireplace. The flames began to come up, and the warmth felt good on this brisk November morning. Sarah came and sat beside him on the hearth, and they talked softly. Sarah was very animated as she began to explain a very disturbing dream. They both agreed that they should have supper for all the people in Somewhere Valley so he and Sarah could relate the unusual events the dream had revealed.

It would be nice if Rob and Lottie could be there, she said, since they had been involved all along, but Rob had said they were coming later in the week. All the plans were made, and at breakfast they asked Tex to invite everyone to their home for a carry-in supper. He had already planned to visit those he hadn't been able to see the last time he went visiting. Jill wanted to go along, and they agreed to be sure everyone heard about the plans.

Work at the Wilsons' place was routine. Carl and Terry were beginning with two new horses and found that they had their work cut out for them. Neither had seen such stubborn animals in a long time. Sarah was to help two young girls learn how to take care of their new horses and get the most out of them. Anxious parents kept calling and offering advice from outside the arena.

Sarah decided to ask them to go to Meeteetse and buy a few items she needed for supper. They left reluctantly, but when they were gone, the girls relaxed, and the training went smoothly. Both girls learned how to lead, saddle, and ride their horses.

By the time the parents returned, Sarah and the girls were riding in the yard and off into the trees behind the Wilsons' house. Golden Girl was a good example for the other horses, and when they came back to the yard, the parents were thrilled at what they saw. They made plans to pick up the horses on Thursday next week. Sarah asked what kind of shelter they had for the horses. Both parents just looked at her. Finally, they admitted they had only a large backyard but no barn or shed for the horses, so Sarah suggested that they wait until they had a place so the horses could be out of the winter weather that would be coming soon.

Riding home late that afternoon was quiet and comfortable for Terry and Sarah until a car nearly ran them off the road and stopped. Terry reached for his pistol, and both horses met stride for stride as they galloped around the car and disappeared into their driveway. They rode around behind the barn into the corral hidden by the aspen grove. They watched for some time, but the car didn't come in, so they put the horses in the barn and ran for the house.

Tex drove in just as they disappeared behind the house and asked about what had happened. Terry had seen the pickup as it disappeared and motioned to Tex to drive around the back. Terry explained what they had seen, so Tex drove out to the county road and looked both directions. He didn't come back for some time. When he returned, he said he didn't see the car they had described.

Neighbors began arriving soon after Tex's return. Sarah was excited and nervous about the information she recalled from her dream. After they had all eaten and were enjoying each other's company, Sarah stood up and told them she had some information that could explain a lot of things and fill in some of the gaps since she had come to Somewhere Valley.

"Last night I had a very disturbing dream. Some things about my family became very clear, but they were also very troubling. I grew up near Cincinnati, probably in the suburbs. I didn't have a sister. I had two brothers. My mother often took in girls who were troubled and needed a start in living right. My full name, which I hadn't even thought about for a long time, is Sallnora Colmbs. My father is Julius Archibald Colmbs. My much older brothers, Archie and Ronnie, were wild, mean, and very disobedient. My father was very rich. He did some kind of manufacturing, probably in a lot of different places, and was gone from home a lot of the time. When he came home, he brought me special things. I don't know where any of them were when I was abducted.

She paused. "I was about twelve years old. I was taken to a strange place out in the country, probably in a different state, where there were a lot of girls just like me. We cried a lot and were beaten and abused by the men who ran the place. I was bought by Sam Rittenhouse to be part of his trade operation. He kept me for his own and often abused me verbally and physically. Jimmy Anson was his bodyguard, and he often used me as his girlfriend when we went on so-called buying trips, probably buying more young girls. Max, the man we caught at our house, wanted me for his own and caused a lot of trouble because Sam wouldn't allow it.

"Max was the one who pushed me out of the car that night here in Somewhere Valley. I can't imagine what would have happened if they had found me or had been able to take me away from Jess and Molly. That is my dream. That is pretty much all of my life. I think it helps to have some perspective for all the trouble I brought to Somewhere Valley. Maybe as we go forward, we will be able to see the end of this long and frightening journey. I felt that you all should know. It also is important because you are my real family now. If the dream is really true, it is even more important for me to be a real part of the Somewhere Valley family. I love you all so much."

Just as Sarah finished, a car drove into the yard. Silence fell on the scene as if a switch had been turned off. No one knew what to expect.

Sheriff Parks checked his gun, went to the side window, and peeked out to see who it was. The tension rose, and everyone became very tense. Some of the men stationed themselves in other parts of the room, ready to act if necessary. In the twilight, he couldn't tell exactly who was out there, but a man and woman were walking toward the front door. He had Terry ready to open the door quickly when the couple knocked, and he stood out of sight. When the door swung open and everyone recognized that it was Rob and Lottie, their appearance took all the tension from the room.

Room for Rob and Lottie was made at the table, and dinner was served to them. As they were eating, Rob said, "I came to see all of you because I have some startling information about Sarah's family." There was a collective gasp from around the table.

"Have I missed something?" Rob asked.

Sarah told her story again. When she finished, Rob was stunned to have much of the same information except that Mr. Colmbs was also missing under strange circumstances and believed to be dead. Neither of the brothers had been found. Sarah's mother had died some years ago shortly after Sally, now called Sarah, had been abducted.

"I am overwhelmed by God's obvious intervention here," Rob said. "For Sarah to have received this dream now and given the events of the past few days, everything fits into a very troubling but also enlightening set of circumstances. I am suggesting that Sarah will no longer be sought to get even or to eliminate her, but someone will try to grab a large part of the estate that may soon become her property. We are facing a very different situation from before."

"I am beginning to understand why the agency sent me and Jill here with such urgency," Tex said softly.

"I don't know who you are," Rob said cautiously. "How do you fit in?"

"I was the first agent that set up equipment to watch the Martin ranch and protect all the other ranchers who could have been in danger or used to get information soon after Sarah was discarded and the agency heard from Sheriff Parks. Jill is the agent who facilitated getting Sarah to the trial for the principal men in the cartel who had originally stolen her."

"You probably don't remember me, since I was usually in the shadows, providing protection. Tex was our Somewhere Valley contact. Getting Sarah to the trial was a very tense time," Jill said.

"I did see you a few times," Rob said

"I am so thankful you were here to help protect us all, Tex," Sarah said

"It is my guess that now the attempts to find Sarah or Sally, as she was called in those days, may not have been to destroy her but possibly will be to use her for a ransom," Sheriff Parks added thoughtfully. "We will probably be fighting a whole different battle and may have been for some time and didn't know it."

"I want to know. Where did you get that man-eating dog?" Lottie asked. "He is an amazing animal, but I wouldn't want to tangle with him."

Sarah told the story of finding him on the porch and how Tex and Terry got him inside. She talked about the weeks that followed while he recovered from his injuries and that he was now their retired military guard dog. Shadow sighed, and everyone laughed.

"How long are you going to be around here this time, Rob?" Jess asked.

"We are going to stay at least two weeks," he said. "I hope to have services in the Somewhere Valley Chapel. It is such a privilege to be here with you. We have wanted to visit everyone again, so it was special finding you all here this evening. There are some tricky legal problems that have come up, so we need to be very careful how we take care of them. I will need some help but don't have any plan for finding it. Hopefully, our visit here will help clear up a number of puzzling questions."

CHAPTER 4

R ob took Terry and Sarah aside and said he had brought several documents that needed their signature, but they could wait until tomorrow.

"We were hoping to be able to stay with you but weren't sure the house was finished. And having electricity must be a real shock. No pun intended. Lights, running water, and all the comforts of home. It is amazing," Lottie said.

"Your room will be at the end of the hall of the left side, across from Tex. I hope you are comfortable," Sarah said.

Rob and Lottie went to the room they were to live in for a few days. They slept well and were awake early, enjoying the freedom from the pressures of Rob's Cody law office, taking care of those in need of legal advice or action. This short vacation was needed, but being able to be in Somewhere Valley was special. When they heard sounds coming from the kitchen, they left their room and settled in front of the fireplace in the great room. Tex came in from a morning walk and shared the fireplace with Rob and Lottie.

"When did you get here?" Rob asked.

"I came last Tuesday," Tex said. "The agency felt it was essential that someone be here to watch for unusual activity that could be missed by people with regular lives and routines. Jill has been assigned here in Somewhere Valley too. She is living with the

Martins because they could be a prime target for information. Both of us are familiar with Somewhere Valley, and we also have a close relationship with the people who are here. There has been some—we call it 'chatter'—that suggests there is renewed and significant interest in Sarah. After last night, we will be putting together a much different plan for taking care of Sarah and all the others in Somewhere Valley, since they are so close to the Martins, where Sarah initially lived, and to Terry and Sarah. Any one of them could be held for ransom or information."

"I was contacted by the Lindermans when they heard that Sam Rittenhouse had died under suspicious circumstances," Rob explained. "They expressed concern, and I believe they were right, that this may in fact change the reason for someone to put pressure on Sarah—not for revenge but for extortion, since she appears to be the only living heir. Her brothers are rumored to be dead, and her mother died shortly after Sarah was kidnapped. Her father, Julius Archibald Colmbs, was also found dead under suspicious circumstances. The whole story is very confusing. The danger posed by her original abductors could be significant now with the probability that she is a multimillionaire."

"I have never been involved in such a complicated situation as this," Tex said. "With the fact that a substantial estate may now rest in Sarah's and probably Terry's hands, who knows what will happen next?" Tex said. "When I first came, it was to try to protect Sarah, then known as Sally when she was under their control, and secondarily her family, and to try to get a line on the mob that was after her. It is much more complicated now, and there is evidence that some of the original cartel are still around. Sarah can probably ID them, so they will probably be even more cautious in trying to abduct her or get information," he said quietly. "Are you going to represent Sarah in what will be a complicated settlement of property?"

"I don't have the time or expertise to take on something of this size and complexity," Rob said. "I have contacted Stan Warner, who is a Linderman relative and a corporate contract lawyer, but he doesn't feel like he is able to take the responsibility either. It is of great concern and needs to be settled soon to protect Sarah and Terry."

"I heard part of your conversation," Sarah said from the kitchen. "I want you all to know that I believe you will find the help you need, and the problems will be correctly settled. I do not want to leave Somewhere Valley. Only God knows what is really best for us, and I am confident you will act wisely."

"Who will do what?" Terry said as he came in to hear the last of the conversation.

Everyone laughed, and Rob explained what they had been talking about. "I don't have a plan for how to sort it all out either. Somewhere Valley is home for you now, and Ohio is a foreign country."

As they were talking, a car drove into the yard. Terry looked out as two men got out and headed toward the front door. "I don't really know what to do," he said.

"You answer the door, and I will stand out of sight, ready to do what is necessary if it comes to be a problem," Tex said.

When the knock came, Terry went toward the door. Shadow was close beside him. Tex called Shadow next to him beside the door as Terry opened it, seeing two well-dressed professional men.

"Good morning. What do you men want?" Terry said nervously.

"We are looking for Sally Colmbs. We were contacted by an Ohio law office regarding the Archibald Colmbs estate and were informed that Sally lives somewhere around here. Can you help us?"

Terry hesitated. "Sally lived around here at one time. I'm not sure why you would want to find her now. But if I hear of anything, I could consult with my attorney and have him contact you. Would that be a help, and do you have some kind of identification?"

"Here is our business card. We have a small law office in Casper and were contacted a few days ago to help with the location and identification of Sally Colmbs. My name is Jordan Richardson, and this is my partner, Will Smith."

"I will have my lawyer contact you if we have any additional information," Terry said. As the men turned to leave, Tex went out to watch them go and got the license number and make and model of their car.

"What do you think?" Terry asked Tex.

"They look legitimate and were very courteous and businesslike, not like most of the people looking for Sally have been."

"I have heard of the firm," Rob said. "This could be a real opening or a dead end leading to more heartache. But it is worth having the contact. I want to go into town this afternoon, talk with Sheriff Parks, and use his secure phone line to make inquiries about these men and call Stan Warner to see if he has a suggestion for help in Ohio."

CHAPTER 5

Terry and Sarah drove to the Wilson ranch to begin their day of training folks and horses to get along with each other and to keep their regular routine and not draw suspicion. Sarah would help a young girl learn how to take care of her horse. No one showed up until nearly ten o'clock in the morning. A man, Mr. Smithson, came and explained that they couldn't take the horse because his wife's daughter had run away.

"Carrie wanted the horse more than she could express, but she didn't want it in a rented stable miles away from home. There was enough room on the three acres of our home, and the horse could live there, and Carrie could ride when she wanted to," he said.

Sarah asked, "Why didn't your girl—Carrie, I think you said was her name—come along today?"

"She ran away two nights ago and hasn't been heard of since. She doesn't like me, and she doesn't get along with her mother. The argument they had exposed bitterness that has been near the surface for a long time. So Carrie left and said she wasn't coming back and hated us both, but frankly, I couldn't care less."

When Sarah heard the story, she nearly cried. The horse Carrie had chosen was a beautiful black-and-gray mare with a white stocking on her left front leg. It was just the touch that made the horse so desirable. The early training had gone well, but Carrie hadn't been near the horse for about three weeks.

"How long has she been gone from home?" Sarah asked.

"She left sometime two nights ago. She is very spoiled and throws a tantrum any time she doesn't get her way, and her mother always sides with her. I can't imagine her taking care of the horse anyway, so if there is some way that I don't have to take her, I would be most happy. I don't have time to mess with her anymore, so it is probably best she is gone."

Sarah was almost in tears while listening to the anger against a girl she had talked to and was sure was very intelligent and caring. She chose to take a chance.

"What is your address?" she asked. "Where do you think Carrie might have gone? Would you be upset if I looked for her and talked to her if I can find her?"

"I don't care what you do with that brat or her disgusting mother!" Mr. Smithson said. "Here is my address. I am leaving for New York this afternoon, and I may not ever come back!" He turned, got in his pickup, and quickly drove off.

Terry was working with a new horse in the training arena. Sarah watched for a while. When Terry saw her, he asked when they would be picking up the pony.

With tears streaming down her face, she told the story. Terry gave his pony the usual treat and came out to hold her close and tell her it was all right. "Not everyone has a good family, and remember, both of us have turned out pretty good. Don't let it get—"

"I want to go look for her!" Sarah interrupted, nearly shouting. "She can't live on the street, and it is just that kind of girl that evil men are looking for. I have her address, and it is only ten o'clock, so I want to go to Cody to find her!"

"I can't see why not, but be careful. This could be very dangerous," Terry warned.

∽∾∾

Sarah left a little faster than she had intended. She wasn't sure where in Cody the address would be, so she asked at the first store she came to. As it happened, it was very close by. Sarah drove to the address. When she saw the house and yard, she was surprised it didn't have two or three horses. It was a beautiful house with a spacious yard, but they weren't what she was looking for. Sarah tried to think of where Carrie would go on a Thursday afternoon.

"She should have been in school," Sarah said aloud. So she drove toward what she thought was a school. It turned out to be a library, so she parked and just waited. It wasn't long before Carrie came out and walked toward Sarah. Sarah prayed for wisdom and stepped out right in front of Carrie.

"You're Carrie Smithson, aren't you?" Sarah asked.

"Uh, why do you want to know?" Carrie said cautiously.

"I was waiting for you to pick up your beautiful pony this morning at the Wilsons' ranch, but your father said you had run away. Can I help you somehow?"

"I don't need your help and especially that man's help! And he *is not my father*!" Carrie answered softly but with anger dripping from every word.

"Well, would you mind just visiting over some lunch with me? I left the ranch after your father did, and I am a little hungry anyway. So let's go get something somewhere, okay?"

"I suppose that would be okay," Carrie said tentatively.

"Good. Where do you want to go? We can do whatever you like," Sarah said.

"I like the Broken Wheel, but it is on the other side of town."

"Suits me. So point the way."

23

The restaurant was nearly empty. The two women headed for a corner table near the back of the dining room. The strangers sat quietly for some time. They ordered and still didn't have much to say.

"Why did you leave home?" Sarah asked.

Carrie became very agitated and glared at Sarah. "If you had to live with my mom and the man she picked up at a party, you would understand why I left. On top of it, I wanted the horse so I could have someone to talk to and be able to be alone with. I can't remember when I was able to talk to my mother, even before Smithson came into our house. All he wants is someone to make him look good. He doesn't care about what he does to anyone else. I have heard it at his office and seen it in the faces of people who work with him. I know he resents my taking up any of my mom's time and doesn't want any interference from me. I won't go back, and I don't expect they, either one, will be looking for me either. You can talk all you want, but I *won't go back!*" Carrie shouted.

"I am not taking you back, if that is what you think. That is your decision. But I want to know where you are going to go. You can't live on the street. I know that from experience. You can't stay with friends forever either. They have lives to live too, maybe equally as hard as yours, and you need to finish school. The hurdles are high for you, and there are a lot of them. Believe me, you need someone to help you. If there is someone looking for a girl who looks lost, you will end up in a very undesirable situation with no way to escape except by dying or constantly feeling like you want to. I know! I have been there, and I don't want you there!" Sarah said softly with as much emotion as she could display.

"So, Miss Problem Solver, what do you suggest?" Carrie shot back sarcastically.

Sarah hesitated. She desperately wanted to help Carrie, but ... She moved around the table, slid into the seat beside the girl, and said cautiously, "I have thought about this all the time I was coming here. That if I could find you and you would agree, I would talk to your mother and ask her to agree that you come home with me. We live on a ranch away from town, where not many people live, but the ones who live there will love you like you have never been loved before. Terry and I will love you too. So, would you be willing to try?" she pleaded with tears in her eyes.

The waitress came with the food and set it in front of them. She hesitated for some time but finally turned and left the two women alone. Carrie munched on her hamburger but said nothing. She took a drink, and Sarah thought there were tears in her eyes. Sarah moved to the other side of the table as Carrie just stared at Sarah for a long time.

"Why would you want to do this? You don't know me or what I am like. You obviously have everything you want. Why would you care what happens to me? I don't deserve it anyway. In fact, if you really knew me, you wouldn't have tried to find me or cared what my mother thinks. You would spit in my face just like I want to do to him and to her. *So why?*"

Tears spilled over Sarah's face as she answered, "Because that is what I was like when Jess and Molly found me and took me in and Terry became my husband. I was ruined merchandise, discarded on a country road, and God rescued me just like I want to rescue you. Please go with me. You have so much to look forward to, and I am sure you will not be disappointed."

Silence hovered over the table so heavy that it seemed to press down on Sarah.

"All right, I'll go with you for one month. Do you understand? *One month!* If you are lying and using me, I will make you so sorry that you will never recover. So if you agree, let's go," Carrie responded angrily.

The young women left the Broken Wheel and went to Carrie's

house. Her mother was the only one home. Carrie explained what she was about to do. She screamed at her mother with the vilest language Sarah had heard since she had been with Sam Rittenhouse. It was very hard for her to hear, but she knew where it had come from. Carrie came out of her room with a small suitcase and walked out the front door without saying anything to her mother.

"I want you to know that I am not stealing your daughter," Sarah said. "I know how much pain she is feeling because I felt that pain when I was merchandise for a prostitution ring, and I know what gave me the willingness to find an answer that satisfied my anger. I will love your daughter like you would, and if someday there is the opportunity to see her again, I can say with confidence that she will not be the same girl. So if you can allow that to happen …" Silence held the two women for some time.

Carrie's mother finally said, "Just get the brat out of my sight."

Sarah said goodbye and left without saying any more. She had thought about seeing Rob and getting his opinion about taking Carrie away from her mother. No one would have loved to have them reconciled more than Sarah, but she left and turned toward home.

The drive home was quiet, which was probably a good thing. When Sarah turned into the Wilsons' lane, Carrie asked whether Sarah lived there.

"No, but I have to pick up my husband. And maybe you would like to see your horse. Your father—I mean, well, whatever he is to you—already paid for him and didn't want a refund. He was just glad to be rid of the nuisance of getting him home and taking care of him. So would you like to see him again?" Sarah asked cautiously.

"I love that horse, but …" Carrie couldn't decide.

As the pickup stopped in the yard near the corral, Carrie

nearly screamed, "There he is! I do want to see him. Can I take him home?"

Sarah heard the word *home* and wanted to praise God, but she softly said, "Yes."

Terry was coming out of the training arena with his student as the pickup stopped in front of the corral. He saw that someone else was in the front seat, so he waited to see what was going to happen as he watched Sarah talk to Carrie.

"Just be quiet," Sarah said. "Move slowly and call his name. You do have a name for him, don't you?"

"I wanted to call him Shadow because of the colors in him," Carrie said. "He is so beautiful. How could I have almost missed this?" Tears streamed down her face.

Both women moved up to the corral, and Shadow came to the gate. Sarah talked softly as Terry strolled up and asked what his name was.

"Shadow," Carrie said.

Carrie was so overwhelmed with her horse that Sarah moved away and talked to Terry about her coming home with her.

"Is that all right? I had to do it. I couldn't call you. Is it okay?" Sarah whispered anxiously.

"If you had asked, I would have said, 'Absolutely.' We have been looking for a Sally for a long time, and I think we have one. I love you," Terry said as he gathered Sarah in his arms.

Sarah noticed Carrie watching from the corral. She knew Carrie expected a lot of shouting and arguing. But as Carrie watched, she saw something that was completely foreign to her experience. Neither adult raised his or her voice in anger. Neither seemed to disagree with the other. There was no stomping or hitting.

She watched as Sarah and Terry turned and walked toward her. She didn't know what to expect and held her pony even tighter, but she realized she had nothing to fear when Terry spoke softly to her.

"I do have a suggestion. If we leave Shadow here for a while and take him home later, you will be able to get settled before you need to help Shadow get settled."

"You want me? You don't know me! You might be sorry I came," Carrie said defiantly.

"I want you in our home as much as Sarah does, and I don't have to know you to know it is the right thing to do. As a matter of fact, I am glad you're here. So let's go home." Terry almost grabbed Carrie and hugged her.

The ride home was quiet as Carrie wondered what she had agreed to. It felt almost too good, and she was sure that in a week, it would all fall apart, just like every other dream she had. When they turned into the aspen break, Carrie began to cry when she realized she was home. The house and barn were so inviting to her, and Shadow gave them a real welcome.

"Let me get out first," Sarah said. "I will introduce you to Shadow. She is usually suspicious of strangers."

Sarah called Carrie to come out and meet Shadow. Shadow nearly smothered Carrie with affection, and Carrie cried again. *What more can happen that feels so good?* she wondered.

Tex came out on the porch, thinking about the recent change in Sarah's status. When he saw Carrie, he thought for sure he knew what had happened and was sure this was Terry and Sarah's first Sally. He came down the steps and greeted Carrie warmly. He wanted to give her the traditional hug but thought it might be a little too much the first time. Carrie couldn't explain it, but for the first time in her life, she felt at home.

Carrie had never been in a log house before. She had seen some on TV westerns, but this was so different. Peace seemed to come from everywhere and surrounded her like a comfortable blanket.

"This will be your private room," Sarah said. "You can arrange it any way you want to, and you can put your clothes in the closet or in the drawers, whatever you want. After you are settled, I will take you on a tour of the house and barn. I think you will like it here very much."

Sarah was sure Carrie was already glad she had decided to come, but there would be hard days ahead too.

CHAPTER 6

When Carrie, Tex, Terry, and Sarah went into the barn, Carrie started to cry. She was so overwhelmed.

"Will I be able to keep Shadow here too?" Carrie asked.

"Yes," Terry said. "But you need to modify his name a little. You see, our dog is Shadow, so your pony might be Shadow II. Shadow II will have a stall all his own, and he will be able to run in the coral with Golden Girl and Traveler. You are at home now."

Tex watched with amazement. He could see the marks of abuse Carrie had endured. Her shyness and questions helped him know she had been hurt, but he also knew she would heal there at the Rocking ST Ranch. He could hardly wait to tell Jill.

"I am hungry!" Terry said loudly. "Let's see what is waiting for us in the house."

As they all turned toward the house, a strange red pickup truck drove into the yard. Sarah grabbed Carrie and ran for the back door. Terry and Tex moved far apart and approached cautiously. No one came got out of the pickup.

As they drew closer, it was obvious that the driver was a woman, and at least two others were in the crew cab. Terry stopped at his pickup and reached for his holster. With the door hiding him, he strapped it on and approached the truck.

When the window came down, Tex came up behind the pickup and crouched near its back door.

Terry called a greeting to the people in the truck. There was no response, so he drew his pistol and demanded that they come out with their hands held high. Still no movement.

Tex opened the back door and nearly dragged one of the men out with one hand. Seeing the man's pistol, he grabbed it and used it to persuade the other two to come out.

Shadow was immediately on guard, growling softly and alert to any movement.

"On the ground!" Tex yelled.

Their no response brought the sound of a gunshot into the air, and the command was immediately obeyed. They were all searched for any other weapons. Now disarmed, the trio still hadn't talked. Tex brought the final back seat man upfront with the other two, and Terry went to his pickup.

Terry keyed the mic. "Terry here. We have three armed, now disarmed and on the ground. They won't say anything, but I am sure they have something to answer for. Over."

"I'm on my way." Sheriff Parks sighed. "Be sure they don't have anything hidden and be careful."

"We know Sally is living here. We just saw her with that other woman. You can't deny it anymore," the woman driver blurted out angrily.

"What do you mean, 'anymore'?" Tex asked.

"We have been here before and ..." They weren't able to say anything else because Tex began to gag all of them with his bandanna and their belts. The third man got Terry's bandanna for his reward.

As Sheriff Parks rounded the corner in his car and came to a stop, he just stared. He couldn't believe the people who had been immobilized and overcome. He had been warned they were very dangerous, but he also felt relief when he saw them where they were.

"Now let's get this straight. What are you looking for?" Sheriff Parks asked one of them as he took off the gag.

"We know Sally is living here. We just saw her, and we want her. There is a price on her head that will make us all very rich, and we can quit this racket. We already told our boss what we have seen, so just watch out. As for keeping us in jail, that won't happen. We have really good lawyers."

"So did Sam Rittenhouse!" Sheriff Parks said sarcastically.

Inside the house, Sarah watched from the window. As she watched, she explained to Carrie why the men carried guns and why they had to be careful all the time.

Carrie was overwhelmed and nearly cried again. "You mean they want to kill you?" she asked.

"I am not sure of all the reasons they want me now," Sarah said softly, "but I'm still able to identify some of the cartel that held me and haven't been caught yet. They may also have another reason: ransom. There are other reasons, but I suspect these want some kind of reward or extortion for their work. I'm not afraid like I was at first when many tried to find me, because I know God is protecting me, and nothing will happen that isn't the way He wants it."

"Are you some kind of religious nutcase? God protecting? And I suppose He even speaks to you. I guess I got myself into more than I bargained for, and you will expect me to say I believe all this nonsense," Carrie said bitterly.

Sarah had expected her attitude sooner or later, so she was ready. "There are no requirements for you to believe as I do— or to believe as Terry or Tex do. All you have to do is take all the love and care we can give you because that is what we have done for others like you. If you want out, I will take you back to Cody next week or any time after that if you feel you haven't been treated right—which reminds me. You will have some responsibilities while you are here, and those will come along as things progress. So just remember that what I said about loving you hasn't changed. Just the location and the circumstances have."

Carrie sat with wet eyes, staring at Sarah and wondering how she could question what had happened.

Sarah saw Sheriff Parks drive in, and all the intruders were being put in his car. She had seen this type of situation before and in much more dangerous situations, but this time the intruders had been caught before they even got their hands on her, so she began fixing supper and asked Carrie to set the table.

"I don't really know how that is supposed to look," Carrie said. "I have never even sat down at a table that had a meal on it, except in a restaurant. But if you show me, I will be glad to help."

Sarah patiently placed one setting, and Carrie did the rest. When she finished, she stood beside Sarah and felt something she had never sensed before: a sense of being useful and helping. When Carrie looked up, Sarah was smiling at her.

"Can you pour some coffee when the men come in?" Sarah asked.

"I have done that before though not with that kind of pot, but I think I can do it."

When the men came in, everything was ready, and Carrie poured the coffee. They reported on what the sheriff had said about their catch.

Carrie sat with wide eyes at the way they talked about life or death so casually. She felt uneasy and again wasn't sure whether coming here had been such a good idea after all.

Tex noticed her concern but waited for a convenient time to explain to her why the strange people were always coming and the tension was happening. *Jill would probably be even more helpful,* he thought.

Carrie slept soundly, even in a strange bed, despite all the troubling things she had seen. As she was dressing the next morning, she heard someone making coffee, so she hurried to the kitchen to see Tex trying to decide how much coffee to put in the percolator. Carrie did her best to help, but neither was sure how the coffee would turn out.

Terry came into the kitchen, poured a cup, sat at the table, and said how much he liked the coffee. Tex winked at Carrie, and she smiled for the first time since she had come.

"I want to do some walking around the place today," Tex said. "Jill will probably need to go with me, but if you would like to tag along, Carrie, I'm sure both of us would enjoy your company."

"When are you going?" Carrie asked.

"I was thinking this afternoon would be nice. It should be a little warmer, and tomorrow I want to go with Sarah and Terry to find a horse to ride. So is that something you might like, either one or both?"

"I would like that. Who is Jill?" Carrie asked.

"She is one of my closest friends," Sarah said. "She has helped me in so many ways to get where I am now, and you will really like her. But she is one tough cookie too." She laughed.

"Carrie, you need to go to the Wilsons' sometime soon and get really acquainted with Shadow II," Terry said. "We would have more time in a whole day. There is a lot to learn, and there's a big responsibility in having a horse of your own."

It was decided. Tex and Carrie went over the hill to the Martins' ranch to pick Jill up after lunch. Carrie met Jess and Molly and fell in love with them right away. Jill and Carrie started toward the rock as Tex explained to Jess Martin how Carrie had come to Somewhere Valley.

CHAPTER 6

Tex and Jill had intended to walk down to the Bar J from the top of the hill and check on possible places where someone could hide. But as they went toward the trail with Carrie, Tex noticed what looked like an old campfire in a hidden place behind a rock. Someone had built a fire there not more than two or three days ago.

"Why would someone have a camp here?" Carrie asked. "It doesn't seem like a very good place to camp, and a rock isn't very soft to sleep on."

"It may be because of what they could see from here. Look over that way. What do you see?" Jill said.

"I see the Martins' ranch," Carrie said

"Now look that way, and what do you see?"

"I see a road that goes behind that hill, but I don't know where it goes."

"Now if you look over that way, you see the top of Terry and Sarah's house," Tex said. "If you move just a little closer, you can see the whole yard. If you wanted to watch for who was living there, wouldn't this be a good place to camp? No one would see your fire if you kept it small, and you could watch a lot of people going and coming."

"I guess that is right, but why do they want to know who is there?" Carrie said.

"If someone was looking for where you were living and suspected it was at Terry's ranch but wasn't really sure," Jill said, "they could watch from here, but they could also watch the Martins and the road into the Bar J. So we think someone who was looking for a person they haven't been able to find for sure would feel that this spot would help find them."

"But why?" Carrie asked.

"Maybe they want to hurt that person, kidnap that person, or kill that person but don't want to be caught," Tex said, "so they watch for a few days or longer to find out what happens at those places and how often they see the person they are trying to find. When they think they have it figured out and how to do it without getting caught, they try. Maybe that was why the people we saw yesterday didn't get out of their truck. Maybe our being there didn't fit the pattern, and they got caught."

"Do you think they wanted to find *me*?" Carrie said thoughtfully.

"No, I am sure they are trying to get Sarah, but we don't know why for sure," Jill said.

The conversation went on for some time as the three sat and watched all that was happening at the Martin and Lund ranches.

The events of the morning made Carrie become even more curious about why Sarah had looked for her and asked her to come home with her. She felt the love Sarah had poured out on her when they had lunch and saw the strength Sarah had when she had confronted Carrie's mother. The fact that Carrie had agreed to come and was here now brought tears to her eyes.

With all the danger Sarah must be in, she still wanted to help me! Even when Sarah knew I could be a real problem if something were to happen and I would be in the way, she still wanted me. I don't understand it, but I want to stay. I want to be as strong as Sarah and Terry are.

"Why do you think Sarah wanted me to come home with her?" Carrie asked.

"Sarah has suffered a lot of pain and fear in her own life, and she wants to give someone else the gift of peace and healing she didn't have before she came to Somewhere Valley," Jill said softly. "Both Sarah and Terry had looked for real meaning for a long time and found it here, and they want to give it to everyone they can."

Jill smoothed back a lock of Carrie's bangs. "I think Sarah felt you had probably been abused for a long time. The way your mother's partner talked to Sarah at the Wilson ranch told her that this could be someone who really wants to be taken care of and wants to find the peace Sarah has, so she searched for you and really rescued you."

She paused, the bright sun making her squint deepen. "Tex wanted you to go with us today to find out that a lot of people here are going to want to love you and care for you so you will become a beautiful lady and may someday be able to help someone else. I hope that makes sense to you."

Carrie sat quietly with tears streaming down her face. She felt something very special in the woman who had searched for her and brought her home, but she hadn't expected anything this amazing.

"Let's go on down to the Martins' place on the back way," Tex said. "It is a nice walk, and maybe we will see something else that might help sometime."

The walk was quite long, and they came up the pasture to the Martin ranch yard late in the afternoon. Jess was working in the barn, so they stopped in to see what he was doing.

"This is a surprise," Jess said. "I'm just trying to convince this colt that a halter is nothing to be afraid of. I don't know if I am doing it quite the best way, but there isn't any hurry, and he will learn it sometime. How is it that I have the honor of such a distinguished company?"

Jess laughed, and everyone joined in.

Jess smiled and glanced at Carrie. "Molly told me we had a visitor to Somewhere Valley, and this must be that lady. My name is Jess Martin, and I am pleased to meet you. I hope you find Somewhere Valley as satisfying as all of us have."

"Thank you. I hope so too," Carrie said shyly.

"We better go and get something for lunch," Tex said.

"I don't think you have to do that, I am sure, but I will check on it. Molly would be happy to have you all for dinner. So let's go on up to the house."

Molly had apparently seen the wanderers strolling out of the pasture through the window and was about to call them to come and have dinner.

The conversation around the table was comfortable. No one asked why Carrie was in Somewhere Valley. She was just included in the family.

"I don't suppose you have met any of the other families yet, have you, Carrie?" Molly asked

"I just got here last night, and Tex and Jill have taken me around the ranch today," Carrie answered.

"News travels fast," Tex said, "and I wouldn't be surprised that most of the people already know you are here. It isn't hard to become one of the Somewhere Valley folks. It just happens, and you're in just like that."

"Did Sarah get her Golden Girl home last week?" Jill asked Tex.

"She sure did. It makes the barn a little less empty. I hope to find a horse for me soon too. I may have to pay rent on a stall, but it is a small price to pay for living in Somewhere Valley." He paused. "We need to get home, but thanks for lunch."

∽◦∾

As Tex and Carrie went down the hill into the Lund yard, a car drove in that Tex didn't recognize. Carrie ran on ahead as the car stopped, but she didn't run fast enough. A woman jumped out and grabbed her.

Carrie screamed and tried to get away but was unable to. Tex moved closer and yelled, "Let go of her."

"I have her, and I won't let go. Sally is what I came for, so just back off, or I will hurt this little witch."

"I'm not Sally!" Carrie cried. When her reply didn't seem to help, Carrie slumped in the woman's arms and stomped on her toe. The grip weakened enough for Carrie to wiggle out.

Tex covered the last few steps, grabbed the woman, and called for Carrie to let Shadow out of the house. When the big dog appeared and charged toward the woman, she gave up, and Tex tied her hands behind her back.

"Go back to the Martin ranch and have Jess call Sheriff Parks," Tex said to Carrie.

"I'm on my way!" Carrie yelled as she ran toward the hill.

Not more than ten minutes passed before Jess, Molly, and Carrie drove into the yard. Jess jumped out with his pistol in hand. "Need any help?" he asked Tex.

"We just need to wait for Sheriff Parks now and turn over our latest captive to him," Tex said calmly.

Carrie began to understand what they had found on the mountain and how it could have been different. She began to understand why the woman had thought she was Sally. There were a hundred more questions, but they could wait.

Sheriff Parks turned into the yard and saw the woman. He shook his head. "They never learn," he said softly. "Where is Sarah?"

Tex just shook his head and said nothing.

They put the woman in the police car's cage and left her to yell and swear. Tex explained the situation, and Sheriff Parks just smiled. "It was bound to happen sooner or later. I'm glad to see it."

Tex introduced Carrie. The sheriff told her how fortunate she was to be here. Carrie just nodded, trying to hide her tears.

"Well, I better get this one on the road to the big house," the sheriff said. "I will have the car picked up tomorrow to see if we can find any clues. Be safe." He turned and drove away.

CHAPTER 7

Tex wasn't sure what to do next. Carrie just stood at a distance with tears running down her face. Tex knew they needed some kind of distraction, so he suggested they go into the barn and see the horses. Carrie moved toward him, and they went into the barn together.

"Have you been around horses very much?" Tex asked.

"Not really. I was supposed to get a horse, but my mom's boyfriend didn't want it, and—"

"Why did you want a horse?" He wasn't sure where this was going, but it was small talk.

"No one at my house really loved me. A friend had a horse, and she said it was so good, and she could talk to the horse about all her problems. It just seemed to me that this was a good idea."

"I want to get a horse too. It is only two, so maybe we could drive out to Carl's place and look together. Maybe you could even help me find a horse. Would you want to do that?"

"I suppose so, but we don't have a car, do we?" Carrie said.

Tex broke out laughing, and Carrie began to laugh too. The new friends just stood there, looking at each other.

"Well, that does present a problem," Tex said. "Have you talked to either of Terry and Sarah's horses? They are really wonderful listeners, I'm sure. We could try to get acquainted if you want to. What do you think?"

"They are really beautiful. Maybe they would like to be in the corral and run around some. Could we let them do that?"

"We could ask them." He laughed.

Both went up to the door of one of the stalls. Golden Girl came toward the door but stopped before either of the strangers could touch her. They just looked at each other.

"Golden Girl is Sarah's horse," Tex said. "It took a long time for her to trust Sarah because she had a bad experience with a girl who wanted her before and didn't treat her very well. Sarah worked hard to win Golden Girl's trust. You may find a horse, but sometimes you have to work hard to get it to trust you. Do you think you could do that?"

"What did Sarah do?" Carrie asked.

"I was there a few times when she had been able to talk to the horse without it running away from her, but she told the horse how much she loved her, and I think she had some treats later on too. Sometimes it's hard to trust someone when others have treated you bad and you aren't quite sure what a new friend might do. But it's always good to try to find the things the other person wants. Maybe you could just put out your hand toward Golden Girl and see if she will trust you by coming a little closer."

Carrie held out her hand and said, "Golden Girl, you are a beautiful horse. I know you can't be my horse, but I want to be your friend. Could we be friends and share secrets?"

Golden Girl stood still. Carrie still held out her hand, and Golden moved a little closer. Not close enough to be touched but closer. Tex moved away from Carrie a little, and Golden came a little closer. When about an arm's length separated the two, Golden turned and went to the other side of the stall.

Tex turned away when he saw Carrie trying to hide her tears, but she just stood there, still with her hand out toward Golden Girl.

No one spoke. The silence was broken when Traveler shifted in his stall and came to the window. Golden moved a little closer to Carrie. Carrie changed hands; her arm just couldn't hold up any longer. The motion didn't seem to change Golden Girl. She move closer and sniffed Carrie's hand.

Tex watched as Carrie nearly shouted, but she held it in as she spoke softly. "Golden Girl, you and I could be good friends, can't we? Someday I hope to have a pony like you, and maybe you and Sarah and I could go for rides."

Golden Girl came close enough to touch Carrie's hand. Carrie was almost afraid to touch her, but when Golden Girl moved close enough for Carrie to touch her neck, Carrie felt that being here was going to be all right. She touched Golden Girl's neck and stroked it gently. Tears ran down her face. "I have a friend who doesn't care what I am but likes being close enough to let me tell her how much I love her. Thank you, Golden Girl. I will come back again."

Golden Girl came to the door of her stall and watched Tex and Carrie leave the barn.

Tex felt something he hadn't for a long time. He wanted to wrap his arms around Carrie and tell her how proud he was of her. He didn't know whether that was all right to do but didn't have to decide because Carrie wrapped her arms around him and cried big sobs of relief.

Tex held her to him. "Hey, it's going to be all right."

They were standing in the middle of the yard when Terry and Sarah turned in. Terry saw them first and stopped to watch. Sarah looked too and watched the pouring out of mutual care and friendship.

Sarah turned to Terry and give him a hug, her heart singing loudly. She whispered to him, "I think we just saw a real step of trust and admiration. I think Carrie is going to make it just fine. Thank You, God, for this special blessing."

When Tex knew for sure Terry and Sarah were watching, he turned toward them. When Carrie saw them, she came running toward the pickup. "This has been a wonderful day," she said. "Jill and Tex were wonderful, and I learned a lot. That car belongs to a mean woman who tried to take me, but Tex and I captured her, and the sheriff has her now. We went to the barn and talked to Golden Girl and Traveler. Golden girl let me touch her. Oh, Sarah, this is the happiest day I have had in a long time. Thank you for bringing me here. I want—"

But she never finished because Sarah engulfed her in a warm and encouraging embrace. "Let's get something to eat for supper," Sarah said. "You can tell me all about it. It has been a good day."

"I also decided when we were talking to the horses that I want to call my horse 'Smoky.' I think it is better," Carrie said. The two walked hand in hand toward the house.

Terry quietly stood beside Tex and waited for him to say something.

"I don't know how to thank you for letting me take care of Carrie today. She and Jill hit it off just fine, as I suppose Sarah expected. She wanted to pet the horses. I was a little uneasy about that. I believe Carrie will be able to win Smoky's heart just fine. We talked to Golden Girl for probably twenty minutes, and Golden Girl didn't run away. In fact, she came close enough for Carrie to rub her neck a little. Carrie had as hard a time trusting Golden Girl as Golden Girl did trusting her. I think it was a special time for her. Golden will always be Sarah's horse, but I think Carrie will be a close friend."

Terry just listened and said nothing. It had been a good day all around.

౷

Carrie helped fix supper, pitching in without being told and asking what she could do. Sarah's heart sang since Carrie seemed to be glad she was at the Rocking ST. Carrie was quiet most of the time but seemed to want to say something too.

"How was your day?" Sarah asked

"It was exciting. I must have walked a hundred miles with Jill and Tex. They found a place at the top of the hill someone had been watching us from. At least they think that is the way it was. Then Tex and I went into the barn to see the horses. I wanted to pet them, but he warned me that that might not happen."

She smiled. "I talked to Golden Girl for a long time and held out my hand. I just wanted to touch her. It took a long time for her to come close enough for me to just touch her. I love your horse, Sarah. She is so beautiful. That was when I thought I would rather call my horse 'Smoke' or 'Smoky.' I think it fits better. Shadow was another reason that woman didn't get away with me. I love that dog too. I love you and Terry, and I love Tex and Jill, and I haven't loved anyone for a long time." Carrie stopped talking as the tears spilled out of her eyes.

"Well, I have to tell you, Carrie, that I love you too," Sarah said as she pulled her close. "I am glad you came to be with us for a while. You can stay as long as you want to, but it is up to you. There are so many times when we aren't able to know which way to turn, but you can learn how to make those choices here. You don't have to go along with others to have friends, and you can be happy without friends when you know who you are and how you want to live. So just enjoy learning, living, and being happy." She paused. "Do you want to call the men in for supper?"

Carrie went to the back door and called that supper was ready. When they sat down, Carrie immediately grabbed the serving dish to help herself. Terry just quietly bowed his head as did the other three. Carrie felt like she had done something very bad, but as Terry gave God thanks for the food, for the successful day, for Carrie and God's protection, Carrie quietly set the bowl down and watched what would happen.

When Terry said, "Amen," everyone began serving himself or herself and passing the bowls around. Nothing was said that made Carrie feel she had done anything wrong. It was a good day, and the food tasted even better.

CHAPTER 8

"So when do you want to start going to school?" Sarah said to Carrie. Silence fell around the dinner table. No one said a word; all of them just kept eating.

Carrie wasn't sure what to say or do, so she started to eat too. Nothing more was said, and Carrie thought maybe the question wasn't that important.

Tex said, "I hear that the Meeteetse school has won all kinds of awards for student activities and for excellent teaching. They have a really good football team too. Do you play any kind of sports, Carrie?"

"I tried basketball, but there were four girls who didn't seem to want anyone else on the team if they didn't choose them, so I didn't try anymore. I probably wouldn't have been any good anyway. I never am."

Sarah quickly looked up. "Why do you say that? Have you played before or played on any team?"

"No, I just knew I wouldn't be any good, so why try?" Carrie answered.

Nothing more was said about sports, but Terry asked what subject she liked most.

"I don't like school, *period*!" Carrie exploded. "I can't see any purpose for it at all. What are books good for? And math is a real waste of time. There just isn't anything I can see that would be a help to me."

"I will make you a deal," Sarah said. "You go to school and try to understand what the teachers are trying to teach, and we will spend time here at home, trying to make sense out of living, using the information from the lessons. Do that for two months. Then if you still don't see any value in it, we will talk about it again. What do you say?"

"I don't suppose I really have a choice, do I?" Carrie said sullenly.

"Not really here at the beginning," Sarah said, "but I will keep my end of the bargain if you keep yours, and I am sure the men will want to help make meaning of those lessons too. But even if that isn't what you want, you at least have to try it."

"I suppose that is a reasonable deal. When is this experiment going to begin?" Carrie asked.

"I was planning on going to Meeteetse tomorrow," Sarah said softly. "Why not start after breakfast? I think Jordan would be willing to take you to and from school. We will look into that possibility too. Since we are going there today, we better dress for success. Let's look through your things for suitable clothes, and if there aren't any that will qualify, we will have to visit the General Store as part of our trip. What do you think, Terry?"

"Jordan will be glad for the company. I don't know if a girl is what he has in mind, but the trip would be better with company. So yes, I think that should work just fine."

Sarah and Carrie left as soon as they could after breakfast and drove to the General Store in Meeteetse. Sarah asked the clerk what girls were wearing at the high school, and with her recommendation, they bought some new jeans and a nice western shirt for Carrie. Her shoes seemed to be okay for now.

"I know you are feeling like I betrayed you, Carrie," Sarah said, "so it is time to put reality to the test. Let's talk to Sheriff Parks about what is required of children living in this county. He also deals with young people who have the same attitude you have about the value of school, and Sheriff Arnie Parks is a good friend who will be straight with you and will support you when you need it most."

Sheriff Parks was sitting at his desk when Carrie and Sarah came in. "To what do I owe the privilege of welcoming one of my best friends and someone I expect will also be another of my best friends?" he said.

"I want you to get to know Carrie," Sarah said. "As you know, she came here under unusual circumstances, so getting to know you as a friend but also someone who really cares about everyone around Meeteetse should be an asset to her if she were to encounter any kind of trouble. I don't know what that would be yet, but let's not wait until something happens."

"Tell me about yourself," the sheriff said softly. "Where you are from? What do you like in school, and what do you hope your stay with Sarah and Terry will help you do?"

"Sarah is calling the shots, and this is her idea," Carrie said sarcastically. "I am only interested in getting away from my mom and her husband. I don't like school. I am afraid of the police. I don't like being pushed around, and Sarah gave me the chance to live with her as an alternative. I like Tex and Jill, who I met yesterday. Terry seems to be a reasonable man, but he agrees with Sarah on what I need to do, and I may not want to do what she wants. So mostly I am escaping my mom and her other."

"Wow!" the sheriff said. Then he sat quietly and looked at Carrie. "Well, let's try an experiment, okay?"

"I suppose so," Carrie said.

"Come over here with me." He led Carrie into one of the cells; then he backed out, shut the door, and locked it. "How does that feel?"

Tears erupted in Carrie's eyes, and she sat on the cot. "Are you going to leave me in here?"

"From what you said, it is probably the safest place for you right now," Sheriff Parks said. "I have shed tears for many young people who have your attitude about life and living when I have put them in that cell. I know that they are only beginning to find out what a life without purpose and a wholesome outlook will bring them, and it won't be long until my cell won't be severe enough to fit their actions."

He rubbed his chin thoughtfully. "You are a good-looking girl who could become anything anyone would want. A doctor, a good secretary in a large firm, a mother who cares—or you could end up seeing the sunlight between bars for the rest of your life. Sarah can tell you how that works on the receiving end of people with your attitude about life."

He sighed. "I know Sarah and Terry must love you a lot and are taking a terrible chance they won't be disappointed. So I suggest that this experiment with crime's consequences be your only encounter with it."

Sarah prayed that Carrie would see the dark side of rebellion and decide to at least take a chance that there might be more to life.

Carrie was quiet for what seemed a long time. She knew other kids who had been in trouble, and she knew how her mother was being treated by the man who lived with her. She was afraid of what she could become, but she was also so uncertain of her ability to succeed. She had never thought carefully up to now, but ...

Sheriff Parks opened the door. "Let's give it another try," he said. He couldn't resist; he drew Carrie into his arms, hugged her, and told her he also would pray for her and help her anytime she needed it to make decisions that didn't come easy.

Sarah and Carrie walked out into the brisk morning, and Sarah put her arm around Carrie. "So do you want to give it all you got?" Sarah asked.

"I don't want to waste my time in jail or try to keep from going there. I'll try!" Carrie said firmly.

∽o∾

The high school was on the edge of town. Students were on a break, so many students were outside when Carrie and Sarah walked toward the office. A few girls asked whether she was going to go to school here. Others just waved. The boys acted like boys, but they were friendly. Students in Cody didn't seem to care whether you were coming or going, and they didn't seem to care whether you were part of their group. Carrie began to feel like maybe school would be okay.

Jordan saw them, took Sarah and Carrie to the office, and introduced them to the secretary. He asked whether Mr. Roberts was in so he could introduce Carrie to him too. The enrollment process took more time than usual because Carrie didn't have any records with her. When the secretary said they would contact the Cody high school for her records, Carrie nearly cried.

"I hope I didn't say anything wrong," the secretary said. "Was there something I did that upset you?"

Sarah explained it was probable that the Cody records wouldn't be very complimentary. She asked whether they could talk to the principal so Carrie's unusual circumstances could be explained fully. Mr. Roberts came to the desk when the secretary called, introduced himself, and invited them into his office. Carrie had been in a principal's office too many times to feel comfortable there. Mr. Roberts saw Carrie was nervously changing positions. He sensed that her coming was also very unusual.

"We want to let you know the unusual circumstances that brought Carrie to our community," Sarah began to explain. "There is no reason to let you guess why Carrie is here without her parents. The truth is not pretty. The circumstances of my being involved

51

are very unusual, but I want to stand with Carrie, absolutely stand with her to see her be able to have a good experience with learning here. Carrie's mother was abandoned with a warning by a man who wasn't her husband and may be engaged in questionable activity. Carrie had run away from home when I found her in Cody, which is where she lived. Carrie had wanted a horse, but her mother didn't want it, and the man who lived there said yes only because he didn't want Carrie to keep bothering him. I suppose you know that I live in Somewhere Valley?"

"Yes," Mr. Roberts replied. "I was there when your home was blown to pieces, and many of us helped build the barn for Jess and Molly. My wife and I have been at the Somewhere Valley Church, known as 'Ronnie's barn,' a few times. I have a pretty good idea of the tragedy Carrie has endured. We have students here who are from other districts and have had much the same kind of home life, and they have become some of our most outstanding students and athletes."

He turned to Carrie with compassionate eyes. "Carrie, you don't have to tell anyone about your past. You don't need to apologize for what you have done or been subjected to, because many of us here have seen what those things did to students. But we have also been able to see what this school and the teachers here have been able to inspire these students to do. You aren't alone anymore. You have Sarah and Terry, but you now have us for your family. I can't think of anyone who won't want you to be a friend or participate in all kinds of activities. You are welcome here. Let me call one of the teachers and the counselor, who can help you get settled in."

Mr. Roberts left the office, and Sarah and Carrie sat quietly.

"So, what do you think so far, Carrie? Want to give it a serious try?" Sarah asked.

"I have never been in the principal's office when I wasn't yelled at and told how worthless I was. I can't imagine this would ever happen. But if I end up here, I have the feeling that I would get some help to go on, but ..." Carrie didn't finish the sentence as the principal and two teachers came in.

"Carrie, this is Mrs. Young. She will be your homeroom teacher for English," Mr. Roberts said.

Mrs. Young smiled at Carrie and went to her. "I think for the first few days, you will stay with me to get acquainted with the school and other students. You won't have to try to find all the classrooms by yourself, and also I can get an idea of what you are good at."

"This is Miss Parkhurst." Miss Parkhurst smiled at Carrie as Mr. Roberts explained what was to happen. "She is our student services teacher. She will listen to your problem if your dog dies or you hurt your toe kicking the dog. She is also our school nurse, so she can bandage up every scratch, even the ones that happen inside when it hurts and you can't get it out. Between these two, you will become familiar with our school and many of the students. And you are not unique, because many students start just like you are. So get ready for an experience that is like nothing you have ever had."

"Do you want to go with me now?" Miss Parkhurst asked Carrie and smiled.

"I guess so," Carrie said, and the two left the room.

"Will you be picking her up after school?" Mr. Roberts asked.

"I will today, but I think we will arrange for her to ride with Jordan Lund, if that seems okay to you," Molly said.

"Jordan is a leader here at school. He came with a lot of problems too, but I believe the people here are really looking for what a young person can do good instead of remembering how bad they were. That will work out fine, I think."

Sarah left and went toward the pickup. She intended to visit with Beulah Parks for the rest of the day. A man came toward her, and he was between her and the pickup, so Sarah mentally prepared for the worst. She looked for an escape route and hoped she could win.

"Are you Sarah Lund?" the man said.

"Why do you want to know?" Sarah answered.

"I understand you stole Carrie from her mother. You told her you would take care of her. Her mother has filed a criminal charge against you. I am Detective Jones from the Cody police, and I must ask you to come with me."

"And where are you going to take me?" Sarah asked.

"You will go to Cody to stand trial for kidnapping and abusing Carrie."

"I need to make a phone call," Sarah said as calmly as she could. She dialed Sheriff Parks on her cell phone, and he answered.

"I am being held by a man who says he is from the Cody police and is trying to accuse me of kidnapping Carrie. I am in the parking lot."

"Keep talking. I am on my way. Don't let him take you anywhere. Do whatever is needed, but don't let him take you!"

Sarah kept asking questions. The officer grew more aggressive and attempted to move closer to Sarah. He reached for her, but she was ready for his move and kicked him in the shin. The distraction gave her time to turn and run toward the school, screaming.

The man chased her but hadn't counted on her being able to get away. As she ran, she tried to open the car doors. Most were locked, but just as he drew closer, she opened a door and pushed it into his face. He fell and swore as he tried to get up. Sheriff Parks had seen what happened and laughed so hard that he nearly stumbled on the man lying on the ground.

"Don't even try to get up!" Sheriff Parks said sternly. A search of the man's coat uncovered a gun, but there was no identification as a detective, policeman, or any other legitimate law officer.

"Lost again! When are you guys going to learn you can't win

over frontier women. They're just too tough for you milk-toast easterners," Sheriff Parks said. "Let's go. Where is your car?"

"Over there, the black one," the man said. When they reached the car, the license was from Virginia.

Sarah heard Sheriff Parks laughing and looked back. She saw them next to the car she had seen someone drive into the parking lot. The sheriff motioned for her to come and identify the man. Sheriff Parks was still chuckling. The man became even more nervous as Sarah came closer.

Sheriff Parks asked, "Do you want to press charges or—"

"Absolutely. Whatever charges I can file against this man won't even pay for the five years of life he had scared out of me. Just take him away, and if I need to sign something, I will stop by your office before I go home."

Sarah sat in the pickup, prayed for God's peace, and gave thanks for His protection. The whole incident made her angry. She prayed for Carrie again and then drove to the sheriff's office. After signing the complaint, she drove home.

When Sarah was close to the driveway, she saw Tex and Jill were just returning from their daily walks around the area. Sarah sat for a long time in the truck, which made Jill nervous, so she went to the truck as Sarah opened the door.

"What happened?" Jill asked.

Sarah told the story again and included getting Carrie settled in school, her fear that Carrie wouldn't survive there, the arrangement for Jordan to bring Carrie home, and the odd encounter with the fake investigator or whatever he was.

"Can we just have a cup of coffee and try to relax a little?" Jill asked. The three friends relaxed, and peace settled over them. Jill gave thanks for God's protection and Sarah's strength. When Sarah told them about pulling the car door open and knocking the man to the ground, everyone laughed. They laughed even harder when they heard how Sheriff Parks had reacted.

Tex went to pick up Terry at the Wilsons' ranch, while Jill and Sarah went to visit Molly.

CHAPTER 9

No one expected Carrie's reaction when Jordan drove in to take her home. Carrie ran to the house and nearly crashed into Sarah. The smile on her face said a lot about her first day at school. Sarah tried to keep a straight face and asked what had happened.

"I have never felt as foolish as I did today," Carrie said.

Sarah expected the worst and waited quietly.

"The math teacher had started a project with the class, which was to design and build a house. They couldn't use any house plan they had seen. They were supposed to design one that was different and would be a better design for a family of four. I was put in with three boys and two other girls. When I saw what they had already drawn up, I began to understand how they used the numbers to keep everything in order. They called it 'square.' They were even trying to record the cost of all the material and … well, it just finally clicked. Math was a real part of living, and I really started to get interested. In fact, they decided to change one of the rooms they had already drawn because I asked a question that made sense to them. I am so excited."

"Was that all you did today?" Sarah asked.

"I had English class and had a hard time understanding, but everyone was interested, and the more I listened, I began to see there was a reason for all this noun, adjective stuff. I felt included there too," Carrie said quietly. "Even in history and the gym class, everyone included me. I have never felt that way before. I know I always ran with a bunch of kids who hated school, so I was never included, but I didn't see anyone who seemed not to be involved. You may be right about school. And Jordan, wow!"

Terry laughed. "You need to know he is my little brother, and I have to admit he is really a good-looking young man and has really grown up these last two years."

"He is going to pick me up tomorrow morning for school," Carrie said.

When Carrie left to change her clothes, Terry and Sarah had to thank God for His generous gift of encouragement. Even when Sheriff Parks and Beulah drove into the yard, they couldn't take away their excitement.

"I just want to tell you what I found out about the latest capture," Sheriff Parks said. "He wasn't after you, Sarah, but Carrie. It seems as though her mother changed her mind about letting her go, so this guy rented a car, which explains the license plates, and borrowed a gun and a fake badge. He was so scared when I put him in the cell that he told me everything. But he may also have connections that might help with events in Ohio."

Terry's phone rang. It was Rob, so he explained that Sheriff Parks was there, and he put the call on speaker.

"I hope no one else will hear this," Rob began.

Terry interrupted, "Let us get into another room to be private."

"Thanks for doing that," Rob said. "I called the law firm in Casper, and both of them are legitimate legal practitioners. I believe they may be Christ followers too. We are going to meet next week in Thermopolis. I suggested their wives could come along, and Lottie wouldn't be alone while we work. I also talked with Stan and have a lead on a law firm that may be able to help us there. I feel as though there is hope for some progress in finding out just what Sarah's situation really is, but as of now, it appears that she is CEO of a multibillion-dollar conglomerate. Is Tex there? I need to alert him to the changed possibilities too."

"If you hold, I will get him and Jill too," Sarah said.

Tex and Jill were sitting on the front porch. They had heard enough about Carrie's description of her first day at school that it seemed to make the job of caring for her even better.

Sarah found them and called them into the sunroom. As they listened to the latest events, they felt the burden shift and the purpose of their mission become even more important.

"We make an evening call every day to our supervisors," Jill said. "They may already have some of this, but we will fill them in with these detail. I think it would be good to mention Carrie and some of the suspicious events and people in her life too."

Everyone agreed.

"We are meeting with the Casper lawyers Monday through Wednesday next week," Rob said. "If you think of us, pray for our wisdom and right contacts. By the way, who is the girl from Cody?"

"I am not sure of her last name," Sarah said. "Her circumstances are very hazy. I felt the evil the moment I went to her house, and I feel quite sure her mother's significant other is even more questionable, maybe even part of the same outfit we are dealing with. I will call you later with the address I have for her. Carrie's first day at school seems to have been an unqualified success so far."

"I'll look into it," Rob said and hung up.

Everyone was silent for some time with his or her own thoughts. Jill sensed that something was brewing. Maybe it was for the better, but it would take even more careful living to be ready. They heard Carrie calling for Sarah, so she left the room, and the others left one at a time to avoid suggesting something was wrong.

Jordan picked up Carrie at 7:15 the next morning. Tex had been waiting for him, and while they waited for Carrie, he told Jordan about the need for caution. Jordan had already known about all the trouble surrounding Sarah, so he wasn't surprised that there could be trouble for him and Carrie. He had hidden a pistol in the car just in case, where it wouldn't likely be found, but for him it was very accessible. Tex was impressed with his hiding place.

Carrie came out, all ready to go, and jumped in the pickup. Tex said goodbye to both of the young people and watched the truck disappear down the road.

Carrie was beginning to find out that school had challenges, but it also had rewards. She found a real desire to learn as she discovered that most learning from books really did have meaning in life. After English class, where they read a sad story about a boy who had been abused, she was quiet on her way to her next class.

"I could have been that boy," she said to herself. "I made the worst decision I could have made when I ran away from home. But if it hadn't been for Sarah, I, well, I might not even be alive now. I know what my mom's man was up to, and it could have been me he took next. I have to tell Sarah as soon as possible!"

"What are you talking about?" her friend Ginny asked as they went into the classroom.

"Just something I need to tell Sarah when I get home," Carrie said, evading the question.

The math project was coming to an end, and excitement was high. Each group had some secret weapon to use in trying to win the honor of having designed and furnished its house best in many ways. Each group leader presented its group's project.

The teacher had invited an architect and an engineer to evaluate the presented plans. When all but Carrie's group had presented, they felt as though they hadn't done enough, but they encouraged one another that their ideas were better than those of the others. They had no way of knowing the outcome, which would be given tomorrow. The teacher and his architect friends would evaluate what all the groups had presented and award the honor of the winning house then. All of them left class quietly. They were holding their breaths, not sure whether they had done their best.

All Friday morning the group members saw each other in the hall and asked whether anyone had heard anything about the results, but no one had.

Just before math class, an announcement came over the intercom for all classes to meet in the auditorium for a special presentation after the second afternoon hour. No one knew what was about to happen. The math projects were hidden behind the stage curtain. Mr. Larkin called the students to order and told them why they had decided to meet in the auditorium.

As the math teacher began to describe the math-required project, the students became quiet. Everyone was excited to know how the results would turn out. Then the curtain was opened, and all four buildings were shown. The engineer and the architect he had invited to help evaluate the results went on the stage with the teacher. They described every project in detail and gave very encouraging description of each. Then it came time to tell which group had constructed the chosen house and why it was the winner.

The final project was Carrie's group. As the architect began to describe the benefits of their design, it became clear that it would be the winner. The contractor had encouraging remarks but said it would be difficult to construct without special skills. The math teacher, the architect, and the contractor had picked Carrie's group as the winner because of one thing.

When the group leader was called up to receive the award, he said, "We didn't even have any idea that was possible, but Carrie had seen it in a magazine and had seen pictures of the idea on a television program. So we redesigned the house to include her idea."

The auditorium exploded into cheers and clapping. The winning group went on the stage and received the prize. A picture of their house and their group would be on display. Also, all the other groups received the same prize, except the winning design would be submitted to an architectural magazine as a house for the future. Everyone in the math class felt as though he or she had won. Later, it was decided that each design had some unique, beneficial features, so all the projects were printed in the same magazine.

Carrie was so overwhelmed that she hid and cried. She felt that she had wasted so much of her time, but because of the terrible situation and Sarah's recognition of worth, she had begun to see how important being a student could be. And she started to see that a road ahead that could give her a fulfilling future.

Soon Jordan and Carrie were on the road home. Jordan just looked over at Carrie and smiled. He knew how he had once felt about school and figured she had felt the same way when she came to Somewhere Valley. He also felt something else for this girl. He knew how Terry and Sarah had looked for someone to help like they had, and maybe this was it.

He began to tell her the story of Sarah coming to Somewhere Valley. As he told her more, Carrie's eyes filled with tears, which ran down her cheeks. Jordan knew just how she felt because he had felt the same when he came to Somewhere Valley with his mom. During the rest of the way home, the two unlikely friends were drawn together. Their future looked even brighter than before, and God smiled.

There were excitement and rejoicing around the Lund table at the Rocking ST ranch. Not only did Carrie make it clear that she really liked school, but everyone was invited to the spring program, where she would sing in the chorus. So much had become so wonderful so fast; they almost forgot about the cloud of uncertainty that hovered over them. Both sets of circumstances gave them all a reason not only for caution but also for hope.

CHAPTER 10

Rob had reserved rooms for themselves and the Casper attorneys in a beautiful hotel in Thermopolis near the hot springs. He reserved a conference room for their workspace and asked that coffee, cold soft drinks, and snacks be provided. His briefcase was full of material he had collected, and he hoped the three attorneys could begin to help make sense of past events and formulate a reasonable plan for the future.

Jonathan and his wife, Evie, arrived a little after three o'clock in the afternoon. Will came by himself because he'd had another call on the way and arrived shortly afterward. When they had all settled in their rooms, Rob called everyone to meet in the large conference room.

"I see our time together as extremely important," Rob said. He gave a brief outline of what had happened and how Sarah had come to Somewhere Valley. Jonathon Richardson watched his wife, Evie, as the tears ran down her cheek, and she wiped them away. He just hugged her and told her it was all right. The entire group spent some time laying out the direction they wanted to take and then decided to go to a restaurant for dinner.

The restaurant they chose had only two other couples in it when the group arrived. The owner greeted them and said he had their table set up as requested and led them to a large table near the back of the room. The time around the table was filled with stories of how they had found their wives, how Will had managed to escape being married, and the joys and trials of law school. They began to talk about Sarah later in the evening. The owner finally came and asked whether they were about to leave since he would like to close.

"I am so sorry!" Will said as he reached for the ticket. "We are in a high-pressure situation, and this is such a lovely place. We just felt quite at home."

The owner apologized but also felt even more privileged to serve this group when he saw the exceptionally generous tip added to the ticket.

Everyone on the team was tired and went to his or her room. Rob and Lottie talked long into the night. Lottie felt the weight of responsibility as much as Rob did. Rob prayed for the rest of the week before they fell asleep and woke early, feeling refreshed. Their early-morning walk was a good wake up, and they met Will out on his morning run. They had breakfast together in the hotel coffee shop.

As the men went to the conference room to work, the ladies left to go shopping

"I believe the first thing we have to do is list all of what we already know and our want-to-know list," Rob said and told the story with more detail, from the beginning and how he had become acquainted with the Somewhere Valley folks and the outcome of their work. He told them how Terry had come and how Sally, now Sarah, had come and how she had been taken into the Martin home. He talked about having the attempts on all their lives, losing their home, being apart for some time, hiding, and finding the support of all the other ranchers in Somewhere Valley. Rob described details of the trial and his part in them as he had helped Sarah in the loneliness and fear she had endured.

When Rob finished, Will and Jon, as Jonathon preferred,

were even more determined that this situation would be solved and done right. In the next two hours, they prayed together often and read portions of the Bible that seemed to help make sense of each situation.

The second morning, Rob suggested that they focus on finding competent help in Ohio. Since the Colmbs empire no longer had Archibald to oversee the operation, they supposed the responsibility would fall to Sarah.

"We had a call from a lawyer in Ohio, asking us to help in solving this situation," Jon said. "I don't remember his name, but he said Stan Warner had asked him to inquire. Maybe Stan would know someone who could help."

"Stan is a close friend," Rob said. "He is a brother-in-law to one of our residents in Somewhere Valley. He would be a good resource. He is a corporate attorney though not one who deals with estate problems, but he may just know of someone who does. Let's call him and see if he can help."

"I agree," Will said.

So they called Stan.

"I had been thinking about Sarah as soon as we heard about the tragedy of Mr. Colmbs. We don't handle corporate actions but have used a legal firm in Columbus who does. I would be willing to call and see what they can do for us and call you back," Stan said.

"Please do," all three men responded.

While they waited, they listed all the items they felt they would need help with. The biggest problem was how to deal with the shady operation they had heard of. How would that be taken care of? How would the daily operation be kept going until changes could be made for supervision and more importantly ownership and many more unknown, unsolvable circumstances?

When the phone rang, Rob hesitated, then answered. "This is Rob Evans. May I help you?"

"Well, it may be more of a question of how I can help you," a woman said. "I hope my answering doesn't present a problem, but I was contacted by Stan Warner to see if I could help with a problem you have. My name is Cynthia Martindale. "

"If you are asking if your reply as a woman is a problem," Will Smith said, "our client is a young woman, and it just may be that you will be a significant help."

"Can you give me some idea of what you are dealing with?" Cynthia asked. "My name again is Cynthia Martindale, and I work with a large firm in Columbus, Ohio. We are all followers of the Lord Jesus Christ and will not tolerate any type of action that isn't worthy of God's name. We are usually involved in very large legal situations with corporations that threaten to ruin the individuals in their companies. So if you could give me some idea of what you are talking about, maybe we can work together."

Rob outlined the situation with Sarah, including her abduction, how she had been discarded, what she had become as well as her family, both in Somewhere Valley and with Julius Archibald Colmbs and his wife and her brothers. Having heard of his death and that of his sons and wife, he emphasized the need to make some determination of what was to be done with whatever holdings Mr. Colmbs had and who owned them now.

"That is a big order," Cynthia said. "I don't know a lot about Colmbs Industries, but they have manufacturing operations, research facilities, and a pharmaceutical and construction company. Some have accused them of very shady business practices, but our past limited contact hasn't revealed anything to cause significant concern. If you are interested in my help, I will send you my résumé, a statement of my fees, and my personal credentials."

"Please do send," Jon said. "An outline of your fee structure and your general credential for the kind of problem we are facing would be helpful, and we will respond, but up to now we can't find anything to keep us from working together."

Both Rob and Will voiced their agreement.

"If you have text ability, I will send them in a return message," Cynthia answered.

The text came through a few minutes later, and as the men looked over Cynthia's credentials, they were even more impressed with her as a partner in this important task. Her fees were just what they would expect from such a highly credentialed lawyer, so they replied that they would welcome her on their team.

Considerable time was spent outlining the next steps. The three men emphasized the danger Sarah was in and that protection was being provided both locally and by the agency. When they finished sharing all their information, answering questions, and establishing an outline of the task ahead, Rob suggested they make contact again the next morning and get some rest overnight.

Time in the Thermopolis mineral pools and a comfortable bed made the team ready for morning and a day filled with surprises and the ever-increasing hope of success. As the men assembled, the ladies went shopping. The morning sun seemed brighter. As Rob, Will, Jon, and Cynthia began putting together their plan, it became clear that as much research as they could do would make seeing the situation firsthand more important. As unexpected as that was, the logistics of getting the necessary people there felt nearly impossible.

"I can't think of anyone in Somewhere Valley who shouldn't know all there is to know and see the circumstances themselves," Rob said. "We have some very successful retired businessmen, and they may have some ideas of what should be done and the right kind of choices. I wonder if Harry has any resource he could use to make this happen."

"Who is Harry?" Will and Jon said together.

"Harry is one of the Linderman clan. He is living on the original family home place, the Bar J Ranch. *But* he has a very successful heavy construction company and probably other contacts that might be helpful. In fact, his bookkeeper, who is now his wife, lived in Ohio. I think he also has a large ranch somewhere near Cleveland. I will call him tonight and find out what his idea might be. It will probably be bigger than anything we would come up with. He is just like that."

"When are you coming home?" Harry asked Rob when they talked later that night.

"Tomorrow morning," Rob answered.

"Come by here, and I will have an idea for you by then," Harry said. "Talk to you then."

Everyone left for home the next morning. The drive for Rob and Lottie was filled with anticipation. As they came near Meeteetse, Rob pulled off the road and suggested they pray for the future and the arrangements that would be made. They prayed for some time. When a local rancher stopped and asked whether they were having trouble, they said they believed God would take care of it since that was why they had stopped. The rancher agreed that a lot of problems could be solved only by God, and he wished them success on their journey. When Rob and Lottie reached Terry's gate, Lottie gave additional praise for God's provision.

"We may get to meet Carrie. She would be the first 'Sally' for Somewhere Valley, wouldn't she?" Lottie said. Rob nodded and drove into the yard. Shadow greeted them with his commanding bark, and they waited for someone to come out to rescue them.

Tex and Carrie came out on the porch. Tex called for the visitors to come on it. Shadow barked his agreement.

"Terry and Sarah went over to the Martins' place and should be back soon," Tex explained. "What brings you here this late in the day?"

"We have some business with Harry, and as late as it is, we decided we would try to find a place to stay overnight. We just came from Thermopolis and the meeting with the attorneys from Casper and a new attorney from Ohio, by phone of course. Things look very promising."

Terry and Sarah drove in just then and greeted their visitors.

"Why are you here so late?" Sarah said. "I hope you aren't going to try to go home after whatever you're here for. Why don't you just stay overnight and go home in the morning? You look pretty tired anyway."

Sitting around the table with a cup of coffee or hot chocolate, Rob outlined what they had accomplished.

"So exactly why are you here?" Tex asked Rob again.

"I need to talk to Harry about some details we need to work out on the case. He might just have the ideas and resources we need to be successful. *And* I won't tell you anymore," Rob said, laughing.

"You could call him and arrange to meet him, or you might miss him," Terry said.

"I didn't even remember you had phone service. So can I use your phone?" Rob asked.

Terry gave him his cell phone, and Rob went outside and called Harry. Harry was so excited. He said he had all but made the arrangements, and "everyone in Somewhere Valley should go along because all of us have been involved all along." Rob suggested that he would call him back in the morning after thinking about it overnight, but it was an exciting idea.

CHAPTER 11

Rob woke early and slipped out for an early-morning walk. He climbed the mountain behind the ranch site and walked along the ridge into the forest. A cold wind made it necessary to have a heavy coat, and sitting was not an option for long. Rob laughed aloud, thinking of Harry's extravagant proposal. Still there would definitely be a benefit for everyone to see for himself or herself what Sarah and Terry were facing. The problem would be taking care of the property and animals while everyone was gone. With no one around, not only would the animals be at risk, but property and possessions would be vulnerable to anyone who wanted them.

Rob started talking to himself aloud. "I suppose Harry has thought of all that too. He usually has almost everything figured out ahead of time. Where will we stay when we get to Ohio? It will be a very expensive proposition to get us there and have a place for everyone to stay. Will it be profitable to do it, or will it be better if just a few go? I can't figure out what to do, but I better get back before someone thinks I'm in trouble or someone has stolen me."

The walk down the hill toward the hay field pasture was beautiful. Most of the aspen trees had lost every leaf, but some were still hanging on. As Rob walked on the path through the aspen break, he spotted someone near the barn, who seemed to be looking for something. Rob tried to see how big the person was but was unable to unless he could get closer. He stopped behind some bushes and watched for some time. When the person disappeared around the end of the barn, Rob ran as fast as he could toward the front door of the house.

Apparently the prowler hadn't seen or heard him as he disappeared around the front of the house and tried the locked front door. He pounded on the door, and Shadow began barking. Terry came to the door with a pistol in hand. When he saw Rob, he shouted, "What—"

Rob yelled that he had seen someone near the back of the barn, apparently trying to get in.

Terry ran to Tex's room and pounded on the door, but there was no response. When Terry opened the door, he saw Tex wasn't there, and he raced to the window. Looking toward the barn, he saw Tex near the back of the barn, looking for something in the grass. Terry closed the door to Tex's room and went to his own, pulled on his boots, grabbed a coat from the rack, and went out. Tex saw Terry and Shadow running toward him and called out.

"I am wondering just what kind of animal made this track here in the soft dirt near the storeroom door," Tex said. Neither of the men had to wait long until Shadow barked loudly and raced off into the aspen grove. A bobcat went up a nearby tree, with Shadow standing guard at the bottom.

Rob came up to the two men and asked, "Did you find who it was that was beside the barn?" Neither Terry nor Tex answered. "I saw someone right there this morning when I came back from my walk. I saw the bobcat, but it wasn't near the ground. Someone was standing near that door. He couldn't have just disappeared."

"I was out here about an hour ago and wandered through the aspens," Tex said. "I didn't see you, Rob, or anyone else. You may have seen me near the barn, but I don't think so."

All the men began searching near the barn. They found Tex's

footprints and began looking for a different set of impressions, but there were no other prints. Tex was surprised that he didn't see Rob walking through the trees. The mystery wasn't solved by the bobcat either.

"Let's make a wide search through this side of the aspens from the middle trail. We can spread out and come this way, and maybe we will pick up another set of footprints."

After they had gone all the way through the aspens to the base of the mountain, no one saw anything suspicious until Terry called from the other side of the barn.

Sure enough, footprints were definitely visible, and it seemed they were headed toward the front door. Tex went toward the door, Terry went around to the back door by the tack room, and Rob kept watch from the other side of the barn to see whether anyone was moving in that direction.

Terry and Shadow went into the tack room, making a lot of noise. Shadow growled softly, and Terry turned to see someone trying to hide behind the saddles. Terry set Shadow on guard and went into the rest of the barn. He saw nothing unusual and called Tex to come in. Both men went to the tack room and saw a boy crowded into a corner, with Shadow in front of him, growling softly.

"You better get that animal out of here!" the boy yelled. "He is dangerous!"

"Only to people like you who are where they aren't supposed to be," Terry said sternly. "You have no business being in my barn, so come on out of there."

Shadow watched the boy move toward him and edge around the big dog. When he was away from Shadow, he became even more arrogant. Tex took him by the arm and led him out of the room into the runway, where the light was better.

"This is the same kid who was here before, isn't it?" Tex said.

"He doesn't seem to learn very fast or remember his time in jail, so maybe it should be longer this time, maybe a year or so."

"I want a lawyer," the boy said belligerently.

"I'm an attorney. How can I help you?" Rob said quietly.

The boy just stared at the three men and said nothing. As they left the barn with the boy, Sheriff Parks drove into the yard. "I see you found the scoundrel," he said. "I heard from the General Store that someone had tried to break in a few nights ago, and the tracks seemed to be about the size of the fugitive I arrested some time ago. I suspected he might go this way. Still, twenty-eight miles isn't easy to cover in a day and night. So, what do you want done with him?"

"We were about to have breakfast, so maybe you could join us, and we can discuss it over some eggs and bacon," Terry suggested. "I wouldn't be at all surprised if this kid is hungry too. What do you say?"

"Sounds good to me. Let me call Beulah to let her know where I am, and we can convene our make-do court and try to decide the best sentence for a repeat offender," Sheriff Parks said, grinning.

Sarah was surprised by the visitors but just put more bacon and eggs in the frying pan without even asking what was going on. Carrie rearranged the plates on the table for the two visitors. When they sat down to eat, the boy reached for the plate to take some bacon for himself. Sheriff Parks grabbed his hand in a firm, probably painful, grip.

Terry gave thanks for the food, and the food was passed around, but Sheriff Parks skipped the offender. When everyone else had been served, he put an egg and two strips of bacon on the boy's plate and said, "Eat! And do it silently. Court is now in session."

Rob took over and asked what charges were being brought.

"Breaking and entering, Your Honor," Terry said.

"Do you have witnesses?"

Tex spoke up. "We do, Your Honor."

Each of the men testified to the facts of the case including where the intruder had been found.

"Does the defendant have anything to say?" Rob asked.

"You bet I do. They have a vicious dog that should be taken care of. These men also didn't treat me right. They hurt my arm when they dragged me out of the barn."

"Were you in *your* barn?" Rob asked.

The boy turned red with embarrassment. "No. I was in *their* barn, but I didn't hurt anything."

"The fact remains that you were trespassing and were in a barn that didn't belong to you," Rob said sternly. "And now you are blaming the owner for the way he treated you? Would you have done the same as he did? Give a vagrant breakfast, keep him warm, and not shoot him on sight? What did you expect the owner to do, especially since you have been here before?"

"I was just doing my job!" the boy said loudly.

"Who hired you to enter a private citizen's property?" Rob asked.

"The same guy who did it before, only this time he said if I didn't do what he wanted, he would dispose of me 'cause I would be a problem to him, and I was just a runaway kid who didn't amount to much anyway."

"Where did you see this man?" Sheriff Parks asked.

"Just before you get into Meeteetse."

"What was his car like?" Sheriff Parks said.

"The same as last time you put me in jail."

Sheriff Parks excused himself, went out to his patrol car, and keyed the radio. When the dispatcher answered, he gave the description of the car and the man and woman in it.

The dispatcher replied, "We have the car and the man and

woman in custody for a speeding violation. Do you want them detained?"

"Absolutely. They are implicated in a much more serious situation. I will not be in my office for a couple of hours, but we can talk then. Thanks for the help. Out." Sheriff Parks went back in to see the end of the trial and prepare for the sentencing.

He had just sat down when there was a knock at the door. Terry went to the door and found Ronnie Moore ready to knock again.

"Come in," Terry said. "We just finished breakfast, and the trial is over. The judge is just about to sentence the defendant."

Ronnie came in with a puzzled look. He didn't understand anything he had heard but was silent as he watched.

"The defendant will stand up!" Rob said. "Has the jury come to a verdict?"

"Yes, Your Honor," those around the table answered.

"We find the defendant guilty of the repeat offenses of entering others' property with intent to harm," Terry said. "We recommend that he be sentenced to one month of hard labor for his offense, with a review of his case after that time and the recommendation of the jailor to be considered."

"And where is this criminal to be incarcerated?"

"Your Honor," Ronnie said as he began to understand the situation, "I would like to confer with an attorney, but it is my intention to take the defendant into my care and see that this lawbreaker learns what is the right way to behave and the value of living to help and not to harm. He will be required to participate in biblical instruction as long as he is in my care." Ronnie finished with tears in his eyes. "I have to go talk to LaVerne, but I am sure I will be back to take custody. Can you wait?"

"We sure can!" everyone said.

Ronnie was out the door much faster than he had come in.

Everyone at the table was talking at once except the boy and Carrie.

"What is going on here?" Carrie asked. "This kid broke the law, and you want to give him to your neighbor. He should be in jail until he rots."

Sarah pulled Carrie into her arms and explained, "When I came here, my real name was Sally. I changed my name to Sarah, because I was a fugitive and had been taken in by the Martins, and I didn't want to remember my past. Ever since then, others in Somewhere Valley have been looking for a 'Sally' to help become a real person. Ronnie and LaVerne Moore, who live across the road, have been looking for a Sally for a long time now, and this seems to be the right time."

Sheriff Parks excused himself from the table and went outside. He had to shed a tear and give thanks to God for the people in Somewhere Valley. He didn't know of anyone else who would even consider a "Sally." Maybe in Meeteetse but nowhere else that he knew of. It was a great day.

Ronnie, LaVerne, and Little Ron appeared not more than twenty minutes later. Both adults had tears in their eyes, and Little Ron was laughing and jumping up and down.

Ronnie sat down beside the fugitive. "What is your name?" he asked.

"My name is, well, they call me Horrty."

"Then, Horrty, would you be willing to live with us and learn what it is like to be a real man with a real purpose and not always be trying to be a bigshot? I know God can make a fine man out of you just like he did for me, so what do you say? If you agree and the judge and sheriff agree, would you do it?"

The silence seemed long, and everyone hoped Horrty would

make the right choice. Horrty sat silently. Finally, he said, "It might be better than jail, so yes, I would give it a try."

"Then it is settled. Horrty will be remanded to the custody of Ronnie and LaVerne for one month. If at that time either party or both decide that this 'Sally' cannot be trusted, Horrty will be taken to jail and tried in court for his crimes," Rob proclaimed.

Carrie saw and heard all that had happened, but she couldn't understand why anyone would want such a brat in his or her home. She could see that this kid wasn't worth trying to change. She was convinced that he would always be the same. As she wondered about this matter, the thought came to her that she had been rescued from a situation much the same, though she had never been caught, and now she also had a chance to become a woman of integrity just like Sarah. She threw her arms around Sarah and said loudly, "I want to be a Sally too. I am not worthy of it any more than Horrty is, but Sarah and Terry have taken me in, and I want to become a real woman, not a fugitive."

A song broke out from all those around the table. Tex wished Jill had been there, but she would hear about it as soon as they met at the rock for their daily briefing.

CHAPTER 12

Rob called Harry and asked him and Janet to come to the Lunds' place to discuss the plans for a trip to Ohio, related to settling Sarah's probable inheritance. Harry was so excited that he nearly yelled that he would be there within twenty minutes. Rob quickly related the results of the meeting with the Casper lawyers and Cynthia. He would also ask Tex to have Jill come over to meet with everyone and help make plans. And they waited for Harry.

Tex went to the hill and saw Jill on her way to their rendezvous. He quickly related what was happening as they went down the mountain.

Harry drove into the yard just as Tex came in with Jill.

The meeting began with Rob reporting all that had been discussed with the Casper lawyers. He assured everyone that the two men were real assets in the search for solutions here in Somewhere Valley. He talked about Cynthia Martindale and her law firm in Columbus, where she was a partner attorney. Rob outlined the discussion that had brought them to the conclusion that going to Ohio was about the only way to really understand the situation and to make reasonable plans for oversight of the corporation Sarah would probably inherit.

"That is why Harry is here this morning. It is my feeling—and Harry said it right away—that as many of the Somewhere Valley ranchers that can go should, because everything that has happened surrounding Sarah has affected them too, and it may even be more important now than before. So Harry, what do you have to report?"

"Well, I have chartered a plane from Casper to Cincinnati. There is not a specific date yet, but there will be a plane ready when we want to go. The plane will be large enough for all the Somewhere Valley folks and Sheriff Parks and Beulah to go with us. I have a large farm north of Cincinnati, which would put us close to Dayton, the headquarters of the Colmbs corporate office. My house has ten bedrooms, and some other rooms can also be used. I already have full-time staff there, so they would be able to provide for all of us. Including the plane, there would be no charge to use my facilities for lodging or meals. We would land at a private airport, which wouldn't draw attention to our coming or going, and I would provide transportation for everyone to my farm and for any visits necessary to factories, et cetera."

"I don't know much about this kind of operation," Sarah said. "But it just doesn't seem right for you to do this. And how will everything be protected here at home and all the chores done, with milking, feeding, and so forth? I don't see how any of us can really go and not put our places here in danger."

"I'm not sure the Wilsons will be able or want to go," Terry said. "Carl has a full schedule for lookers and training. I can take our horses there, so that would be one less burden. But let us find out who would be able to go and who would rather just stay here to help out. It is a marvelous opportunity to see Harry's farm, but the trip may not work out for everyone. Is there a time limit when we can go?"

"As far as I am concerned, anytime is the right time," Harry said. "I have five top hands working for me at the Bar J. They take care of all the livestock, and they also live right there. They could easily cut some of the work they do there and spread it among all the ranches. They know how to do everything and are good at it, and I know they are honest and trustworthy. It is October, and everything will slow down toward winter anyway. So you decide. Janet and I will act according to your wishes. I probably should go there anyway and check up on my company, but don't let that be a part of your decision."

"Well, it seems as though we need to talk to all the people who might be involved first," Rob said. "And I need to get home and tie up some loose ends before I can go along, which I feel is essential. Let's plan to go in three weeks. That should be enough time to put all our business in order. Does that sound reasonable?" Everyone agreed and went out to begin the work necessary to make such a trip.

Every person in Somewhere Valley had had some part in protecting Sarah and helping with various chores and responsibilities at very dangerous times, especially during the trial. Most of them had business backgrounds and could be helpful in knowing what to look for in each of the sites in the Colmbs empire. Everyone was given the choice to be included.

Terry, Sarah, and Tex decided to go together to make arrangements. The Youngs had been involved in taking care of Sarah and Molly during the house episode, and they were definitely interested in helping to bring Sarah's life into focus.

"I am glad the Youngs want to go," Terry said. "Paul has a lot of business experience and may be helpful in seeing problems the rest of us may not. I wonder what the McNerneys will want to do. I can't see them being interested in big businesses or maybe even in traveling, but I want them to go."

After Sarah explained the situation, Leona was interested but very much afraid of flying. Jim couldn't see how he could make any difference if he was there or not.

"Where did you say this trip is going?" Jim asked.

"We will be at Harry's farm near Cincinnati."

"Cincinnati, you say? We just may be interested after all but not only to help Sarah. One of our sons lives by Dayton, and we just may be able to get him to want to see us. We haven't seen him or any of his family for years, and he don't seem to care much at all. Once in a while, we get a Christmas card from him but not often. Yes, we just may be interested—that is, if we weren't just takin' advantage of a trip at a good price."

Terry's answer was enthusiastic. "I don't see any reason it wouldn't work. You would have to work out your own transportation and would need to be at the airport when we decide to leave, or you might just be living in Ohio. How can you find out if your son would be interested in having you come and could come and pick you up and bring you back?"

"Can we call him on these newfangled telephones we got?" Leona asked.

"You sure can, if you know their telephone number," Sarah said. "And it won't cost you anything to do it either."

Both McNerneys were surprised and said they would try to reach him today.

The next place to visit was John and Veda Mae Fisher's place, which brought an enthusiastic yes. "We want to help any way we can, and since you are near our son, we may want to try to at least see them. We also want to support you as much as we can. You say Harry has an airplane he can use for this?"

"Well, he has arranged for one, but it isn't his. He will rent one to use," Tex explained.

"If we need to help pay for that, we will be glad to help," John said.

"It is all taken care of," Sarah said. "When Harry wants to do something, he wants others to get a lot of happiness from it, and he doesn't care how much it costs. So you are on the list."

As they drove toward the Moores' place, Sarah was very quiet.

She had wondered whether she would soon be able to provide this trip on her own, with Terry approving, of course. If she was going to own all this wealth, she wanted it to work for others, more than just for her family. She didn't say anything to anyone, but she would be talking to Rob as soon as possible.

Ronnie and LaVerne were so excited when they heard about the trip, but neither felt it was the right time to go, since Horrty had just come to live with them. The adjustments had been a challenge, but neither Ronnie nor LaVerne could keep from smiling. Little Ron didn't understand yet, but they were sure Horrty would be a good brother when he began to see what a family was really like. They generously offered to help take care of all the places that would be vacant.

"We will be at every place at least two times each day and make sure nothing is happening that shouldn't be," Ronnie said. "We know about how each of our neighbors does things, and we can do them almost the same. I wonder how Harry will make out with his spread. He has a lot invested there."

"He says his men will be just as good workers when he is gone as when he is there, and they would probably be able to help out with other places that will be needing attention. I think he is probably right," Tex said. "I have gone over there, and Harry or Janet aren't anywhere around, but the men are working. They know when they have a good thing, I think."

The last stop was the Wilsons' ranch. Terry was nervous about how Carl would feel about him being gone. He wasn't at all sure either of them would want to go along. Carl and Caroline had become close friends in many ways. Carl was putting a horse back in the big corral as they drove into the yard. He gave a friendly wave and finished his job before coming to talk.

"This must be important to have all of you here at once, or do you want to buy a horse?" Carl said, laughing.

"I do want to buy a horse but not today," Tex said. "The reason we came is probably more important than buying a horse right now."

"With such important business, we should have a cup of coffee, and I am sure Carol will have some kind of goody to go around. She keeps me kind of plump with her baking, so let's find out," Carl said on the way to the house.

When they were all seated around the table, everyone became quiet. Terry explained why they were there. After he finished, the silence lasted for some time. Carl wasn't really surprised that the trip was being planned. Carol understood the importance of seeing everything firsthand, too.

"We aren't trying to pressure you into going along and aren't hoping you will stay home and maybe take care of all our horses," Sarah said. "If there is any way you can go with us, we want you there. You understand so much about what it takes to run a successful business that you may just have the solution we need to manage this enterprise. I don't have any idea what we are going to see or what we don't want to see. But we want our friends who have helped us so much already to be with us, if possible. If you need some time, we have until next week to decide."

"We had wondered what your father built in his collection of different kinds of businesses," Carol said. "And what we have heard about Harry's farm sounds like a resort and not a farm. But Carl and I don't feel we can go." Carol left the conversation hanging. Everyone was silent. No one wanted to break the comfortable outcome that had pulled them together this afternoon.

"The fact is that neither of us is physically able to fly," Carl said. "We want to go, and we could arrange for the time to do it, but we can't be physically flying in an airplane. For some reason, it makes walking very difficult for a long time after we fly. We flew a lot when we lived in Kentucky, buying horses and going to horse shows, but something happened that makes it nearly impossible to get around for three or four days after a flight, and it isn't really cleared up for at least two weeks. So we will be happy to take care of any and all horses from all the ranchers who will be going as our part in the success of this event. And we can help take care of things here while you are gone."

"I have always had a great deal of respect for you, Carl, and you too, Carol. And today only increases that respect," Terry said softly. "I know two special horses that will be able to come back home here. Ronnie and LaVerne will also be staying home because they have a 'Sally' now and don't want to interrupt the adjustments Horrty needs to make."

"Horrty?" Carol said. "Where did they get that name? It will be a magnet for all kinds of problems in school."

"He said his name is Horace, but his mom and dad always called him 'Horrty,'" Sarah explained. "I don't know if you are aware that we also have a "Sally' at our home. She is a girl from Cody. Her father bought a horse for her from your corral but didn't really want to take care of it. I think she may go with us, even though she will miss some school, because I want to keep an eye on her. She wanted that pony with the white stocking foreleg and the gray-and-black body. She is a unique horse, and she wants to change her name from Shadow to Smoky or Smoke. She has a hard time making up her mind."

"Well, we probably should be going on home," Tex said. "We have made the rounds, and it seems as though everything is going to work out just fine."

When they were settled in the pickup on the way home, Tex explained why he felt they needed to go right then. "I just feel like something is happening at home or maybe at the Martins' place, and we should be there to help. I can't seem to shake the feeling either."

Terry drove faster when they turned on the county road. When they were near their gate, he slowed and cautiously turned in just in time to see what looked like a girl running toward the barn and disappearing inside. "Now what?" Terry said as he stopped.

Sarah and Tex jumped out and followed the person into the barn. Just inside the door, they stood silently in the shadow, trying to see where the person had gone. They didn't have to wait long before a girl appeared from the tack room. Sarah stepped into a light in the runway and confronted the girl.

"Just what are you intending to do here?" Sarah asked loudly. Keeping the girl's attention gave Tex a chance to come up behind her and throw his arms around her, holding her as she screamed and struggled to get free. Neither remembered seeing this girl before, but something was familiar about her. Her jeans were dirty, and she obviously hadn't bathed in days. She was about Carrie's age but had a swagger about her that was troubling.

Sarah moved closer and told her to stop struggling since she wouldn't be set free until she had provided some information and an explanation. The girl finally stopped trying to get loose, but Tex still held her. She said nothing as tears ran down her cheeks. Her dirty skin made the streaks of tears even more noticeable.

"You have to tell us what is going on and why you are here," Sarah said. "Where did you come from? Who brought you here? We aren't interested in hurting you, but you have to help us make sense out of your being here."

Finally, the girl nodded, and Tex released her. He stood close by between her and the door. He could catch her if she made a move in either direction.

"Maybe we can sit on that bench and figure out just what is going on," Tex said. Sarah and the girl sat on the bench, and Tex sat on the floor in front of them.

Silence. Terry came into the barn and just stared at the scene before him. He looked at the girl and said, "I saw you yesterday when I was at the General Store. I knew you were stealing candy bars, and I thought you should be in school, but I was in a hurry and forgot all about it. Why are you here? Where did you come from?"

"We have been asking that from the first time we saw her," Tex said. "This girl can't talk, I guess, because she hasn't said a word and acts like she can't. I suppose we will just have to call Sheriff Parks to pick her up, since we aren't going to have the chance to help her. Terry, why don't you go call the sheriff?"

"I'll talk!" the girl said abruptly. "I ran away from home about three weeks ago. My mom is a drug user, and my dad is seldom home. We just moved to Lander, and I didn't like anything there, especially school, so I left. I caught some rides, but the last one wanted more than giving me a ride, so I threatened to jump out if he didn't stop. When he did, I ran into some trees until I heard him drive off. I don't know for sure where that was, but it was around here somewhere 'cause I finally got to Meeteetse. Yes, I took some candy bars, but I was hungry. I slept behind the church last night, even if it was cold. I hoped I could get some help, but nothing happened, and I wandered through town out onto this road. I found your place and tried to find someone. When I knocked on the door, the dog didn't like it and growled and barked. That was when I ran toward the barn. What was I supposed to do? What are you going to do with me now?"

"First, we need a name," Sarah said, putting her arm around the girl. She felt her shaking.

"My name is Rhonda Gibson," the girl said. "So I suppose you can send me back home now that you know who I am. I promise you I will not stay there. I want a lot more than a worthless mother and an absent father. So—"

Despair and anger were so obvious. Sarah put both arms around her and nearly cried.

Terry was trying to figure out how they could take care of another girl and what kind of arrangements would need to be made. How did this fit into the plans for the trip, which was so necessary? Where did they go from here? But nothing seemed to make any sense.

"I am going to see Jill," Tex said abruptly and left the barn. There were no solutions anyone could even imagine.

"Well, let's get you in the house, get you cleaned up, and find something for your tummy," Sarah said. The girl looked at Sarah, surprise written all over her face.

Rhonda began telling a story, which made Terry feel sick. When Carrie came home a short time later, she just sat, watched Rhonda, and listened to her story. Tears came to her eyes, and she hugged Rhonda, telling her she had come to the right place; everything would be all right now. Both girls were crying. Terry and Sarah watched Carrie, who had been a spoiled brat when she came, give herself and her love to a girl she was sure felt a lot like she had.

"I don't know what you did, but it couldn't have been as bad as what I did," Carrie said, tears running down her face. "Sarah and Terry were able to help me see how much I was missing out on, and I know we can help you too. You can sleep in my room. Can't she, Sarah?"

"I suppose we can arrange something," Sarah said. "But right now we need to get some supper ready."

"We can help," Carrie said.

Rhonda wasn't sure just what was happening, but despite the circumstance, she began to feel like there was hope, and she pitched in, peeling potatoes and helping to set the table.

Jill and Tex came in as everyone was sitting down for supper.

More places were set for them, and supper was served. Rhonda began eating as soon as she had some food, but Carrie whispered, "Wait. First, we need to thank God for your coming and for the food." Terry smiled as he thanked God for Rhonda and for the food He had provided for them.

"Lord, we need Your wisdom and direction. Help us to be all You want of us for our girls and others here in Somewhere Valley. Make your direction clear so we can serve You best. Amen."

CHAPTER 13

Terry thought he heard a faint knock at the front door and felt the fear of danger that was often there when someone came unannounced. Pastor and Doris Hastings knocked again, a lot louder this time, just as the evening meal was coming to an end. There were so much laughter and talking that no one else heard the knock at first except Shadow.

One loud bark caused Terry to feel uneasiness as he heard the knock on the door more clearly. He wasn't sure what to do as he went toward the door. Tex came alongside and stood along the wall with Shadow, ready for action.

Terry opened the door and welcomed Pastor Mylon and Doris.

"We were out just driving around, decided to go to Somewhere Valley, and turned in here," Pastor Hastings said. "We don't know exactly why, but it is always good to see our friends. Don't let us interrupt your supper. We will just wait until you finish."

"We were just finishing," Terry said. "But have a seat here while we help clear the table.

"We can do it," Carrie said. "Rhonda and I will wash the dishes. You just visit."

Pastor Hastings looked at Sarah with an unspoken question. While the girls laughed and talked, Sarah quietly shared what had happened. Doris nearly cried for Rhonda as the story unfolded.

"One problem is that we are planning to go to Ohio next

week to try to make sense out of this estate situation, and neither Rhonda nor Carrie fits in. I don't know what we can do now. There isn't time to try to find out about Rhonda's parents and provide for her before we go," Sarah said.

"Could they stay with us? I'm not sure about school, but we could take care of her while you are gone. It would be nice having someone living with us anyway, wouldn't it, Mylon?" Doris said spontaneously.

Sarah just sat quietly. Not a sound came from the kitchen, and both girls were staring at Sarah. *What am I supposed to do now?* Sarah thought. *Is this the answer? Neither of the girls is well known yet, and Rhonda is certainly a problem. The situation is all so sudden, so unexpected, and quite troubling. We don't know anything about Rhonda. She could be real trouble. What do I say?*

Carrie came to the rescue again. "If both of us could stay with the Hastings, I could help Rhonda get settled in school. I know she would really like it here anyway, and I really don't want to miss a whole week."

Sarah and Terry didn't know what to say. Tex and Jill were amazed at the turn of events. No one spoke for a moment.

"If Rhonda wants to stay here," Sarah said, "I could get her into school, and she could probably ride with Jordan just like Carrie is. This is Tuesday, so we would have three days to see how that is going to work out. Are you sure you want two silly teen girls in your house for a week, Doris?"

"We were both teens at one time not too long ago, so I think it would work just fine. We may find out we like it and start looking for a—what do you call it?" Doris said.

"You mean 'a Sally'?" Jill said.

"What is 'a Sally'?" Rhonda asked. "Is it some kind of disease or something?"

"It is a long story for another time," Terry said. "But let's think about this arrangement. It just feels like it may be something God would be waiting to do. We have a few days to decide anyway."

Sarah noticed that Tex and Jill were sitting very close and whispering to each other.

So it was decided that the plan would be considered, and Rhonda would go to school the next morning with Sarah to get enrolled and settled. Carrie was anxious to help her find her way around and get to know some great friends, but she didn't say anything. She wondered whether she really could help, but she wanted to. *I guess I will just have to wait and see.*

Mylon and Doris left and drove home sometime later.

"This had certainly been an unusual visit," Mylon said on the way home.

The discussion about the girls was all their conversation, and by the time they drove up the driveway, they were convinced that God was preparing them for something special.

Harry was excited about being able to make all the arrangements in the plan for the trip to Ohio. He called Sam and Dottie, his caretakers at the farm in Ohio, and told them what to expect. Without hesitation, they said everything would be ready and were looking forward to meeting all the people.

Cynthia Martindale was making plans for their visits to all the work sites. She had contacted the foreman at each location. All of them were excited to meet their new owners, a response that surprised Cynthia somewhat. Usually there was a lot of anxiety with such a huge change. A charter bus was secured that would hold all the visitors. It looked like everything was nearly ready for the great day.

Harry went to see Jim and Leona and asked what they would need to make their visit rewarding. He could have a pickup ready for them to use to drive wherever they wanted, if that would be best.

"That would be nice," Leona said. "But we thought our son could just once come and get us so we didn't get lost. We would like to talk to him but don't know how."

"Do you have his phone number?" Harry asked.

"Yes. So much has happened lately that we aren't even sure of. And we don't know how to use our phones. What do we have to do? Call the operator and get her to place the call or ... well, can you help us?" Leona said.

"So much has happened lately with electricity and phones," Jim said. "We just aren't sure how to act. We have lived here for almost forty years, so the changes are a little bit confusing. It isn't that we don't like them, but we don't know how to use most of it, especially the telephones."

"I sure can help. Let's see, it would be about nine p.m. in Ohio now. Would that be too late?" Harry asked.

"I don't think so," Jim said. "He never liked to go to bed early before. I can't imagine he would now."

Harry dialed the number and switched to speaker. Jim and Leona just sat stunned as the answer came. "Hello?"

No one said anything, and the voice asked, "Is there someone there? Hello!"

Leona said, "Hello, is that you, Harold?"

There was a silence on the line, and Harold answered cautiously, "Mom?"

"Well, don't you recognize your mother's voice anymore?" Jim said abruptly.

"I do, but you have never called me. It is a big surprise. Angie is here too. Where are you?" Harold said.

"We are at home," Leona said. "We just got one of these newfangled phones, and our neighbor is helping us learn how to use it. We are coming to Ohio next week and wondered if we could come and see you."

"This is amazing. Of course, you can come and see us. Where can we pick you up? It will be wonderful for you to be here. We will have all the kids and their families come, and we can have a wonderful time. How long can you stay?" Harold asked.

"We will only be in Ohio a week or so. I will let Harry, our neighbor, tell you where you can come and get us," Leona said with tears running down her cheeks. "Here's Harry. See you soon."

Harry explained when and where they would be coming and where they would be landing and when they would have to leave. He encouraged Harold to come down and meet all the folks one evening if it wasn't too far. Harold thought they could maybe spend a day with them. When all the arrangements were made, Leona and Jim said goodbye, and the call ended.

Harry was so excited that he could hardly contain himself. Jim and Leona had tears of happiness in their eyes. Harry praised God he could help Jim, and Leona and he drove toward home with a song in his heart. He liked making people happy. He had wondered what the trip to Ohio to settle Sarah's problems would be like, but he had never expected to be able to reunite some of his precious Somewhere Valley families with their children.

On the way home, Harry stopped to see John and Veda Mae Fisher, since their house had been Sarah's hiding place when the Martins found her. John met him at the door and invited him in. As they sat around the kitchen table, Harry asked where their family lived. They couldn't remember for sure, but Veda Mae had found a letter postmarked from Richmond, Indiana. Harry said that wasn't more than sixty miles from his farm. He suggested that they might want to invite their son and daughter to come over for an afternoon and evening visit while they were in Ohio.

"We hadn't thought of that, but it might work out. I guess we could call them now," John Fisher said. He got his phone, and Veda Mae looked up the last number they had for their son.

John dialed the number. Fear rose in his throat as the phone started to ring. He recognized his son's wife, Rose, when she answered.

"Rose, this is John Fisher," John said tentatively.

"I don't know a John Fisher," Rose said. "What do you want? What are you selling?"

John had tears in his eyes as he explained that he was Jim's father and that they would be coming to Ohio next week. "We will be less than sixty miles from Richmond and wondered if you would want to come and visit."

John heard Rose calling Jim and telling him what was happening.

"Dad?" Jim said. "What is going on? Is Mom all right? Why are you coming to Ohio?"

John explained briefly what was happening and hoped they could get some time to visit and maybe even have the whole family come to Harry's place some evening and meet all the folks from Somewhere Valley. "You are less than sixty miles from Harry's place, and you would be very welcome, even to stay overnight."

Harry nodded enthusiastically. "Yes!"

"This is amazing!" Jim said. "We just talked about trying to get back together again. Our kids don't even know they have a grandfather and grandmother. I don't think my sister has ever spoken of you since we left either. When will you be here? How will you get here? This is wonderful, and I'm sorry we haven't …" Jim couldn't talk anymore.

Harry took the phone and explained all the details: where they would land, where his farm was, and how to get there.

Jim assured them they would be there with the whole family, and he would see to it that his sister also came.

Harry ended the call with tears in his eyes. John and Veda

Mae talked with Harry for nearly an hour. When Harry left, he had to stop and shout his praise to God for all that had happened.

"This will be a wonderful trip. I just know it! Praise God!" Harry shouted.

When Harry came home, Janet asked him where he had been. When Harry described what had happened and that two families were going to be reunited again in Ohio, both of them had to shout for joy.

Jordan had been studying in his room and raced to the kitchen to find out what was wrong. When Janet explained, he wondered something.

"I wonder if my sister will ever want to contact us again," Jordan said softly.

Janet hadn't thought about it before, so she started looking through some letters she had saved and finally found where Mary had last been and a phone number. She dialed hesitantly, and the phone began to ring. She motioned to Jordan. Just as he came close, there was an answer.

"Hello," an angry voice answered. "If you are selling something, I don't want it, and don't bother me again."

Before Mary had a chance to hang up, Janet said, "Mary?"

The phone was silent, but it wasn't disconnected.

"Mom?" Mary answered tentatively.

Tears came fast for Janet and Jordan. "Yes, it's me and Jordan. How are you?"

"Why are you calling? Are you in trouble? Where are you? What do you want?"

"We just wanted to try to find you again. We are in Wyoming. Jordan is here with me. I am married to a wonderful man and living on a large cattle ranch. How are you, and where are you?"

"I live in Middletown. I have a job cooking in a restaurant. I am by myself. I can't seem to make anything work out anymore. Why are you in Wyoming? What are you doing there anyway?"

Janet explained how she had come to Wyoming and mentioned that Terry was here too. She explained that they were going to Ohio next week and why; she wondered whether they could see her. Harry was standing at the door and listening. When he realized who Janet and Jordan were talking to, he sat down beside Janet.

"I could pick her up someplace," Harry whispered. "She isn't more than ten miles from the farm."

"Can I call you when we get there? Maybe we can get together for a little," Janet said.

"Yeah, Mom, we could. Gotta go. Maybe see you. Bye."

Janet wasn't sure what would happen, but Harry was all excited. "She could work at the farm," he said. "We always need another hand for some reason, especially in the kitchen. Maybe we can work out something. Let's just wait and see!"

Harry slipped out of the house, unnoticed. It was dark, and the yard lights had just come on. He called Terry and told him what had happened and that they would probably see his sister. Terry was glad his sister was all right, but he wasn't sure he wanted to see her after the way she had treated their mother. She had also never wanted to be around him.

"Anyway it would be all right if it happened," he told Harry.

Arriving at school with Rhonda the next morning, Sarah felt the tension rising. She sat quietly for a few moments before moving to go in.

"Is there something wrong?" Rhonda asked.

"No, I was just thinking about the last time I did this with Carrie. Can you tell me something about your school experience? That's because they will be asking where you came from so they can get some records," Sarah said.

"I am sure they won't be happy if they get anything from my school in Lander," Rhonda said. "I am certain Lander High is glad I am not around there anymore after all the trouble I caused. So if it is all the same to you, could you not tell them about Lander? I would like to start fresh, maybe even try to learn something for a change."

Sarah just sat, silently looking at Rhonda. She thought of her high school years as a slave to Sam Rittenhouse, when she had felt like no one cared about her or her feelings. She thought about how the situation had worked out with Carrie. Maybe she could pull it off again, but this time it would probably be harder. They all knew her, and she knew and respected them. Carrie had turned out better than expected, so maybe …

"Well, let's give it a try. I think if you come halfway, the teachers here seem to really like the students in their classes and are determined to help them as much as possible, so what do you think?"

"I can do it," Rhonda said. "But I don't want them to know my family name either. What do you think?"

"We just have to try," Sarah said.

As they approached the front desk, the secretary recognized Sarah and greeted her enthusiastically. "Do you have another lost person for us to enjoy?" she asked, looking at Rhonda.

"I do. I want to be honest with you, but some of the information we have could be troubling and might keep Rhonda from making a fresh start here. Can we talk with the principal for a few minutes?" Sarah asked.

"He will be back in about fifteen minutes, but let's go back to his office, and you can wait there," the receptionist said. "I think he will understand your situation and do what he can to help. As you know, we are committed to helping our students be all they can be." She looked at Rhonda and smiled a genuine welcome smile.

Sarah watched Rhonda as she shifted from one foot to another and knew she wouldn't like the idea of waiting in the principal's office, since that was where bad things happened.

Rhonda tried to picture what the principal would look like— probably rather overweight with a loud voice. He probably has very thick glasses too. She chuckled.

A man came into the office who looked like he had just come from football practice. When he sat behind the desk, Rhonda was really surprised. Mr. Roberts talked softly to Sarah for some time, and she explained how Rhonda had come to her attention.

"We have talked about her going to school and have agreed that it would be best if she did," Sarah said, "but she very much wants her past to stay behind her, even as much as you not knowing her parents, not finding where she came from, or not contacting the school for her records. Rhonda knows it's not likely you can do all this, but maybe we can discuss it and come up with a reasonable solution."

"There are rules and regulations I have to abide by," Mr. Roberts said. "I will have to get her records from her previous school, especially if it's in Wyoming, but I don't have to share those records with anyone unless there is a compelling reason to do so. Also, I really do need a full name. Again, I may not have to contact her parents unless we have a problem of some kind that needs their permission. So, Rhonda, tell me truthfully about all the skeletons in your closet and where that closet is, please."

"I don't want to," Rhonda said.

"I know. I wish I didn't have to ask you to either. But it will help me give you better choices knowing who you are and why you are here instead of at home," Mr. Roberts said.

Rhonda began telling him about the abuse at home. Her father had been absent so much, and her mother had tried to force her to be good. When her father returned, he yelled at her and hit her sometimes, even with his belt buckle.

"I have the scars to prove it. We moved to Lander about a month ago. Right away I did something at school that one of the other girls didn't like, and she told everyone. The boys pinched me. I hit them and knocked them down. The principal put me in detention, which really helped my studies and reputation. So I did nothing but cause trouble until I ran away. Carrie, Sarah's other Sally, told me how wonderful it was here at Meeteetse High School, so I decided to try to learn something and not just be a troublemaker, and that is about it."

"I don't know what you mean by 'Sarah's other Sally,'" Mr. Roberts said.

Sarah explained briefly all that had come about but wasn't sure what anyone else thought about the saying or the title, so she said no more.

Mr. Roberts left the office. When he came back, he said two teachers were coming to the office to talk with Rhonda. One was the gym teacher, and the other was an English teacher.

"These two teachers are some of the craftiest teachers I have. They can find ways to make things happen for students when no one else can, and every other teacher looks up to them for help if they need it," Mr. Roberts explained.

The secretary came in and said Mr. Jones and Mrs. Ripley were here.

"Have them come in," Mr. Roberts said.

The two teachers came in, sat across the room, and watched Rhonda. Mr. Roberts explained the situation. He told them everything Rhonda had said, being clear that it wasn't what Ronda wanted to happen, and asked for their comments and suggestions.

Rhonda expected them to say they didn't want anything to do with her.

"Rhonda, why are you here and not at home?"

Rhonda hesitated.

"I can't help you if I don't know why you chose to do what you did," Mrs. Ripley said.

"I just didn't want to be in trouble at home and at school. Running away felt like getting even, I guess," Rhonda said.

"How has that worked out?" Mr. Jones asked.

"I'm not sure. Sarah says I have to go to school, but I hated school before. Carrie said it was different here, so I, well, maybe, maybe it could be different, but I don't know."

"You are the one who needs to decide," Mr. Jones said softly. "We love our kids here and try to give them every opportunity to succeed in school and how they feel about themselves, others, and their classes. It means you will have to try much harder than many students because you have failed so often, and not all our kids are kind all the time either. So how much are you willing to put into it?"

"I guess if it doesn't work, I could run away again," Rhonda said stubbornly.

"And you will keep on running if you don't do something about it," Mrs. Ripley said. "We have students who were determined to hate school but found out that the one or two things they wanted to do depended on how much they put in, not how much they got out, which turned out to be far more than they expected. So if you're willing, we are!"

"I want to try." Tears came to Rhonda's eyes. "I want to amount to something, so I will try."

"That is all we ask. Also when you have problems, you have to ask for help, not solve all your problems with your fists or your fingernails," Mr. Jones said sternly.

"Okay, let's give it a try. I will share Rhonda's records only with you two and no one else. The first week will be the hardest, so dig in and get ready for a big test of your character. Let's do it!" Mr. Roberts said.

Mrs. Ripley took Rhonda to the classes she would be attending and introduced her to the teachers. She was welcomed warmly. When they came to the math class, Carrie saw her and ran to see whether school was going to work for Rhonda. When Carrie found out Rhonda would be in her class, Carrie gave her a big hug and shouted to the class that her special friend would be coming to class with her. Everyone cheered. Rhonda was overwhelmed.

The day went by fast, and school ended. Jordan picked Carrie up and also learned that Rhonda would be riding with him.

"I'm going to have to charge fares if I get any more passengers," Jordan said, laughing.

CHAPTER 14

Sarah held her breath most of the day, hoping Rhonda would come home in one piece. When Jordan drove into the yard, she went out to welcome them. It was obvious Rhonda was very happy. She jabbered about school all evening and couldn't wait to get there tomorrow. Sarah could hardly believe how much she had changed.

"I think I am the best in my English class and history class. I knew more about all the things they were teaching than it seems anyone else knew, especially history. I have always liked history and read a lot about our history, so that class will be a favorite. Math has never been my best, but my teacher is really great at making it understandable and that it means something important. I think I will be able to succeed. I sure hope so. I don't want to let Mrs. Ripley, Mr. Jones, or Mr. Roberts down," Rhonda said loudly.

"I don't think you will," Carrie said. "You are smart, and you catch on to everything fast. You are better than I am in math, but I am okay there too. I am so glad the first day was so good."

Rhonda even smiled as Carrie talked about her in class.

"Do you think you will be able to fit in with the other kids?" Terry asked.

"I haven't had anyone challenge me like they did in Lander, and I haven't been pushed around like I was there either. Even the girls there were, well, not nice. All they forever talked about were their boyfriends and what they did on dates. I didn't hear any of that here. Everyone just seemed to like everyone else. I am sure some are special to each other, but they aren't hiding in the corners either. It is different here from any place I have ever been. I like it so far. I suppose there will be stuff later on, but for now, it is pretty good. When are you leaving for Ohio?"

"Probably on Monday. We will have to drive to Casper and fly from there," Terry said. "We will take the horses down to the Wilsons' ranch on Saturday. Then we can lock the barn doors, and that should be safe. Tex and Jill will go with us to Ohio, so there won't be a lot of people around. I hope everything will work out well. We will take you and Carrie to Pastor Hastings on Sunday afternoon. You and Carrie will need to look after each other while we are gone."

"I can take care of myself," Rhonda said stubbornly. "I don't need anyone to look after me."

"That is probably true, but just the same, it builds a stronger defense if there are two who stand together in the face of trouble. And there could be trouble for either one of you. Maybe not in school, but that isn't the only place you will be. Neither of you is completely out of the woods for someone to want to take advantage of you being here by yourselves, even if you are staying with Pastor Hastings. Some people are looking for Sally—you know, Sarah—and would probably stop at nothing to get her. So be careful. Don't take chances and be constantly aware that God protects us when we call on Him. This is still a very dangerous time," Terry said softly.

He continued, "Both of you have come into our lives for a reason, and we want to be able to see it through. You know that Carrie didn't exactly come from a very good situation either, and she has been pretty tough about some things too. You will also need to obey Pastor Hastings and Doris. They will have our blessing to be your mother and father while we are gone. If they feel the need for discipline, then we expect you and Carrie to learn from it, not to try to get out of it."

"Are you ready to have supper?" Sarah asked.

"I could eat anything I can get my hands on," Rhonda said. "Going to school did work up an appetite I didn't know I had."

Final preparations were being made, and schedules were assigned for those staying home and checking on all the ranches, the livestock, and the buildings. The five men at the Bar J decided one or two might stay at one of the houses each night and sleep in their pickup. That was a suggestion from Ronnie and Carl. Both of them would come early in the morning to help with any chores that needed to be done, and then they could all go home and sleep for a while in their own beds.

The pattern would change every day. Tex and Jill went to every ranch yard and tested the equipment Tex had installed to provide surveillance for each place. Being connected to all that had happened with Sarah made every place in the valley a target. All the Bar J men and Ronnie were told to check in at one of the cameras every time they went to each place.

CHAPTER 15

Church was a new experience for Carrie and Rhonda. Neither had ever been in church before, and meeting in the Somewhere Valley Chapel was a real surprise. On Sunday morning they wore the one set of clothes they had as they walked across the road to Ronnie's barn.

"Where is the church building?" Carrie asked.

"Right in front of you," Sarah said. "We have met here ever since we conquered the rustlers, and somehow it just feels right to meet in Ronnie and LaVern's barn. We are planning a new chapel on the hill in Somewhere Valley next spring, but this is our church now, and it is special to us."

As the folks sang, Carrie and Rhonda just watched. By the second song, they were joining on the second verse as they caught on to the melody. Neither understood just what they were saying, but there were phrases that stuck in their thoughts.

"On a hill far away stood an old rugged cross."

Now what does that mean? Carrie wondered.

"Oh, How I Love Jesus" made Rhonda think of what love was and how they could love Jesus, who was dead and gone.

"What a friend we have in Jesus, all our sins and griefs to bear."

I don't have any sins that I need someone to carry around for me. I am doing just fine carrying them myself, Rhonda thought and wondered, *What is sin anyway?*

Sheriff Parks stood up and talked about two men who had built houses. One built on the sand, and the other dug down and laid a good foundation to build on. But one day a flood came. "Now how do you suppose the house on top of the ground, the one on the sand, stood up to the floodwaters? You guessed it. The ground was washed out from underneath it, and the house began to lean to one side. The wind came along and finished it off.

"Harry doesn't build our houses on top of the ground. He digs down and puts cement deep down where the rocks are and then builds up from there. Then he puts long bolts in the concrete so that when the logs get here to build the house, they can be fastened to that foundation sitting on the rocks and all that concrete.

"Well, it is just like us building a life. Some of us have said, 'I don't need all that God stuff. I can do it all by myself. I'm tough, too tough to be taken advantage of or beaten. I know how to take care of myself.' So at work the next day, someone does something that hurts you very bad and takes away your job, or you get in an argument that ends in a fight, and you lose or win. What did it do for your reputation and your feelings about yourself? Kinda messes with us, doesn't it? Makes us uncertain about the next time. But if we know we are right and our houses, our lives, are established on God, then we meet the problems, and we can bend and sway but not break. We don't have to prove we are right or stronger. We can be confident that God is our foundation, and He will help us. We may get treated wrong, but God knows what is best, and in the long run we come out like a house built on the rock, which can stand against the wind and the snow and can look just as good after the storm as before. So where are you putting your trust? In the sifting sand of riches, craftiness, strength, or arrogance? Your house will fall someday! But if you have your life built on the truth of the Bible and you intend to live that way, you may lose a battle here and there, but you will ultimately win. So let us trust God even more!"

In the closing song, they sang, "My hope is built on nothing less than Jesus' blood and righteousness." Carrie wanted to know what the words meant. She asked Sarah to explain them. All the way home Sarah explained the meaning, that we can only trust on Jesus. He is the only person who doesn't change or fail. Rhonda felt more uncertain about her ability to solve her own problems, but she wasn't sure about all this faith and Jesus talk either, so she decided she would and see what happened.

CHAPTER 15

On Sunday afternoon Terry and Sarah took Rhonda and Carrie to stay with Pastor Hastings for the week. Both girls had their doubts about staying with the pastor. They had heard enough to raise questions about the church in Ronnie's barn. Rhonda and Carrie felt almost abandoned after Terry and Sarah left. Home for them had never been quite like it had been with Terry and Sarah, and they felt very much alone.

As they talked the situation over in their room, they decided that each one would watch out for the other and try to help avoid problems at the Hastings's place, on the way to and from school, and at school.

"Girls," Doris called, "we like to have popcorn and play a game on Sunday evening, so if you're up to it, come on down and join in."

Carrie thought they might as well have something to do, so they went down to the kitchen and sat around the table. Pastor Mylon set out the giant Scrabble board and asked if they knew how to play the game. Neither girl had ever played any table games, so he explained the simple rules, and everyone drew his or her letters.

Carrie was chosen to play first, and she played "where." Doris played *some* and made it *somewhere*. Rhonda felt uncertain about what to do, so she asked, "I can't play on *somewhere* because I can't think of a word that would be real like *somewhere*, so what do I do?"

Mylon helped her play a word across the word *somewhere* ending in *s*, which gave her a triple-letter score. And so the game progressed. As the board filled up, it became harder to find places and words to play.

Rhonda really liked the game and used every skill she had to remember words from some school subjects. As the letters dwindled and the scores rose, the end of the game came down to Carrie with three letters, and she found a triple-word space that fit. When the scores were added up, both girls had done better than they expected and wanted to play again.

"It is now eight twenty. We can play until nine thirty, but if we aren't quite done, we will add up the scores then and declare a winner," Pastor Mylon said.

"I usually stay up a lot later than nine thirty," Rhonda said. "That is for babies, not grown-up people."

"That may be true, but it is usually our bedtime around ten p.m. so we can get a good start on tomorrow. I have some important meetings with folks tomorrow, and I want to be my best. I don't have a problem staying up later for a good reason either, and it often happens, but let's make ten our goal every night. Okay?" Mylon said firmly.

The game was put away, and everyone went to his or her room. Rhonda quietly sat on her bed. She had never had anyone decide what she should do, and as much as she felt some resentment toward Mylon Hastings for his general rule, it felt like he cared about her, and she couldn't understand why.

"Do you feel like I do?" Ronda said to Carrie. "Just like Sarah and Terry, these people care about us. Why should they? We don't mean that much to them."

"I do," Carrie answered. "But it did feel good for them to

care about us and the people Pastor Mylon will be meeting with tomorrow. I can't remember any time my family ever cared about anyone but themselves. All they wanted was to beat everyone else or take something from them."

"Well, whatever it is and as much as I don't like anyone telling me what to do, you're right. It felt good. So maybe a little extra sleep won't hurt a thing," Ronda said as she slid under her covers.

Despite going to bed early, the girls had to be called the next morning since they were still asleep.

"Breakfast in thirty minutes," Doris said as she knocked on the door, waking both girls.

Pastor Hastings took the girls to school and dropped them off about twenty minutes before their first class. Someone saw them come with the pastor and asked what had happened to Jordan. Neither knew how to answer, so they said the pastor was just helping out today, which was technically true. They remembered that the trip was semisecret and knew not to advertise that the ranchers weren't at home.

School was quite exciting for both girls. Rhonda was able to try out for the volleyball team, and she felt she had a good chance of making it. Carrie decided to try debate, since she liked to argue anyway. Neither girl expected the work it would take to do well, but both put all they had into their preparation and practice. Just before the last class of the day, they met in the hall.

"I can't believe I like school!" Rhonda said. "I have to do well in class to stay on the team, but I can work as hard as anyone, and I think I am going to like it. Are you good in math? I have trouble with some of that stuff."

"I thought debate was just arguing, but it is really hard finding proof that something isn't the way others say it is," Carrie said. "I can't remember a time I didn't argue with my mom, but I didn't really have any reason to be arguing, even when she was right and

I didn't have an answer. This is going to take some real work. It is great!"

The girls parted and hurried to class just before the final bell. After their last class, they met in the hall and realized they weren't sure how they were going to go home. They could walk, but even in a small town, they weren't really sure of where they were going or the best way to get there. They didn't have to wonder long when they saw Doris drive up. It was a good thing she did because a woman had been watching them from the parking lot and followed Doris as she turned onto the street. About halfway home, Doris became very nervous.

"I think we are being followed by that red car," she said. "It has made every turn we have, and I made a lot I didn't have to, trying to find out if they were following us. We are going to the General Store because the sheriff's office is right next door. When we stop, you run into the office and report them. Try to get the license number too."

She turned several times more and ended up in front of the store. The girls saw the office and ran that direction, only to find it locked. As they turned around, they saw the woman and a man coming their way.

"Okay, we need teamwork on this," Rhonda said softly. "When I yell, 'Go,' dive at the man's legs and try to lock your arms around them, and I will do the same for the woman. We may be able to get them on the ground and maybe knock them out in the process. Easy now. Don't act interested yet. So how were classes today?"

"Just great," Carrie replied louder than necessary. "Math was the greatest, but I really got into history too."

"Now!" Rhonda yelled.

Both girls dove at the ankles of the man and woman. Clutching their legs threw them off balance, and they fell backward on the ground, hitting their heads hard. Neither moved, and Rhonda went to the woman's purse and found a gun. Carrie also found a gun in the man's shoulder holster.

"If you can use this, keep him covered while I use my shoestring to tie this woman's legs together," Rhonda said.

Carrie knew enough about guns to know she had to pull back the hammer on a revolver, so she did it as the man sat up.

"There won't be any movement by either of you!" Carrie yelled loudly. "I can use this pistol and will even if you are just trying to sit up, so get back down on the ground!" Both the man and woman complied reluctantly.

A patrolman had just driven up to the office and had watched the whole incident from his patrol car. As the girls were trying to decide what to do with the man and woman, the officer jumped out and ran toward them.

"I will take over now. What is going on here?" he asked sternly.

"These two followed us all over town, so we came here, but no one was home. We did the best we could with what we had, and look what we found on these two. If you want to take over, please do!" Rhonda said and lowered her weapon.

Carrie let the hammer down on her gun and handed it to the policeman. He took the man and woman into the office, searched them thoroughly, and put them in a cell for safekeeping. Then he came back out. As he was closing the door, he asked the girls to get in his car.

"Sorry for putting you in the cage, but I can't get you both in the front seat. Now who are you, and why do you think these people are following you?"

Doris had seen the whole thing from the car. She had intended to get into the store and call for help, but the performance of the girls was stunning. When the patrol car came, she had started toward it, watching the intruders being locked up and everyone

113

getting in the car. Now she tapped on the window, and the officer opened it just far enough to talk.

Carrie said it for her. "That is the lady we are staying with. She did a great job of trying to lose the car but couldn't, so we did what you saw here. Can she sit in the front seat and help explain?"

"Of course," the patrolman said, and Doris got in.

The explanations were a little confusing, but the patrolman said he was filling in for Sheriff Parks. He said their description of what had happened was a good explanation of the situation. "Your presence of mind and Mrs. Hastings actions make a lot of sense. I have to tell you, I wouldn't wonder that you girls could make great law officers someday based on the way you took these people down. I do need all your names and addresses, but you are free to go, and we will have more help here by tomorrow. We will also be patrolling Somewhere Valley more frequently. I have a feeling we will get a lot of information from this couple. So how is school going for you girls?"

"Neither of us ever liked school until now. For me, it is going very good," Carrie said.

"Not liking school wasn't strong enough," Rhonda said. "I hated school and all the people in the three different places I have been. But I don't know just what there is here. It isn't like anything I have ever seen, and I am really liking it too."

Doris just sat quietly and thanked God for a real miracle. "I think we are going to have a great week." She prayed silently.

Driving home, Doris praised God for His help and deliverance. Both girls didn't quite understand what Doris was saying and why she was thanking God because they were the ones who had done everything, but when she said, "I thank You, Lord, for giving Rhonda and Carrie the strength and quick wits in taking down the man and woman," they began to understand what she had meant by her prayer.

When the girls were back at home and had gone to their room, Carrie said, "I never thought of God caring about stuff like today. I figured that if He even existed, He would be so busy with everything else that He couldn't care about or help one person in such a little place as here."

"Up until I came to Somewhere Valley, I never thought there even was a real God. Some of the people I have heard talk about God never seemed to make much sense, and it didn't sound like He was interested in what happened each day," Rhonda said thoughtfully.

The discussion at the supper table made Pastor Hastings shake his head more than once. He said, "Praise God!" so many times Carrie couldn't help laughing aloud.

"Is that all you can say? 'Praise God'?" she asked.

"I have seen some amazing things since I realized that God loved me enough to have Jesus die on a cross to forgive me and put me on a different path, but I can't remember a day recently that had so many good things happen to people I care about. I just know God is at work," Pastor Hastings said. No more was said about the day, but it had made its mark on the Hastings family and both girls. Nothing could change that.

CHAPTER 16

The charter plane touched down at a small but obviously significant executive airport in the Ohio countryside. The excitement and anticipation grew as all of them went into the elaborate terminal. Harry went to the desk and asked when the bus would arrive.

"It should be here any minute. In fact, I think it just drove up," Matty, the receptionist, said. "It is good to see you back in the territory, Harry. I understand you are living in Wyoming now. What on earth is there in Wyoming that would keep you there? We miss you around here."

"I think there are three things, probably more, but three for sure. First, there are the beauty of the mountains and the feel of the place where I started growing up. Second, the people who live there are really one big family, and you will get to meet most of them. Third, I think that is where God wants me to be just now. Good enough?" Harry said, laughing.

"Fine with me, so let's meet your friends."

The attendant was impressed with the rugged, friendly folks from Wyoming. She greeted all of them warmly and told them they were in for a wonderful week at Harry's farm resort. "You must be tired, so let's get you on your way. The bus is just outside, and your bags are already loaded. We look forward to serving you any way we can during your stay."

As the bus left the airport, Sheriff Parks began singing, "Praise God from whom all blessings flow." The words had a special meaning for each person there as he or she faced an unknown that would affect all their lives.

Getting settled at Harry's estate was an experience. The staff had everything ready, and the rooms were all assigned so each family had a private place to rest and be alone. Cynthia Martindale and her husband arrived just after everyone else was settled. Their welcome was just as warm, and they felt at home. Rob had come to the great room just as they came in, and Cynthia greeted him.

"I bet you are Rob Evans," Cynthia said. "I had pictured you nearly as you really are. This is my husband, Art. It is such a privilege to be working with you. Are the other attorneys here as well?"

"They are, and they are anxious to get to work, but I think Harry Linderman has plans for us this evening in getting to know you and the rest of the Linderman family. Oh, here is Sarah now. Sarah, come meet these folks."

"That handshake was enough to assure me that I wouldn't want to tangle with a woman from Wyoming," Art Martindale said, laughing. "It is a pleasure to actually see who Cynthia has been talking about nonstop for the last few weeks."

"Everyone, let's go out to the backyard for some refreshment and a special Ohio barbecue," Harry called.

When everyone was settled, Harry Linderman introduced the rest of the Linderman clan with colorful descriptions for each. All the others introduced themselves, and the food was served. Conversations went many directions with folks getting acquainted and forming friendships. When the food was nearly gone and the sun had graced the sky with a spectacular sunset, Harry called the meeting to order.

"You all know the purpose of our visit. Part of that purpose is to build on the friendship we have experienced so far and make bonds of friendship that will reach across the miles. But Sarah and Terry are most significant here and their family back home." Harry outlined the circumstances of Sarah's coming to Somewhere Valley as Sally, then asked Rob to share all the twists and turns legally, spiritually, and personally that had happened in Somewhere Valley.

Rob told the story of the land ownership again and described how he had met Otis Linderman at church and developed the bond of friendship with whole family, which had grown over the last two years. Rob felt troubled as he also began to relate the specific reason for being in Ohio and why all the folks had come.

"We have been in contact with Cynthia, and she has been wonderful to work with. I want her to share a suggested outline for our visit here. The days ahead are bound to be a challenge, so we definitely need all our strength but especially our prayers as we move ahead," Rob said, concluding his remarks.

There was an interruption before Cynthia could begin. "There is a man here who wants to see John Fisher. And there is woman here who wants to see Leona McNerney," Harry's foreman said. "They are in the great room now if you want to go there." Everyone held his or her breath as John, Veda Mae, Leona, and Jim got up to see children who hadn't contacted them in years. As the couples left the circle, Stan Warner prayed for a blessed reunion and a renewed sense of God's blessing on all of them. Everyone responded with a hearty "Amen!"

Cynthia shared what her law firm had been able to find out about each of the parts of the Colmbs empire. "The house has been sold, but all the other parts are operating as usual. We were surprised to find competent leadership in all the factories and quite well-kept ledgers. Of course, in any enterprise as large and diverse as this one, there are always some parts that are concerning, but overall Colmbs Enterprises appears to be rather well run. We have arranged visits to each location with a thorough tour of each facility and its operations. It will necessitate a very long day, but I believe it would be best to do it that way if possible. Do you have questions?"

Sarah sat quietly, troubled. She felt the burden of responsibility come crashing down on her, but she also felt a strange calmness that seemed to settle on her and around the firepit. Though she wasn't sure just what lay ahead, she knew God would certainly lead her as He had through the twists and turns of living in Somewhere Valley.

"Has there been any kind of will or direction found?" Sarah asked.

"The search of the house and all the papers hasn't revealed any document of that nature. It is customary in this type of situation to rely on establishing a relationship of next of kin. That would be you, Sarah, and a process has been set in motion to settle any and all claims of ownership or attempts of misappropriation. So far, we haven't had any such claims, and we have advertised extensively in that process. In any case, my firm and I want to assure you that your representatives will work together with us to establish legal filing and documents of your ownership and sole responsibility, in cooperation with other advisers as necessary."

Serious discussion went on through the evening.

The tour, scheduled for tomorrow morning early, would be a long day. All of them settled in their comfortable rooms to try to sleep and be rested for the next event. Sarah asked Rob and Lottie to come to their room, and they talked and prayed together. Terry assured Sarah that he would be with her in any decision she might make and would support her completely.

"You know this already!" Sarah said emphatically. "It is not you or me. It is *we*, or have you forgotten again? We have had this conversation before, and it still stands no matter what."

Rob nearly laughed at the strength Sarah exhibited. Instead, he rejoiced in the bond that held them together.

The McNerneys and Fishers made arrangements to visit their families the day after tomorrow and would leave early in the morning and probably not be back until late in the evening. All of them cheered after they made their announcements and wished them well.

CHAPTER 16

The chartered bus left early the next morning as the visits to every facility began. All the folks from Wyoming were well received at each stop. Questions came fast from both sides. Most supervisors were concerned about their position but were assured there was no reason for them to be replaced since it appeared they were doing a good job. It was made clear that Cynthia and her firm would be the overseers with Sarah and Terry as the principal owners. A governing board would be appointed for the final approval of any changes. When the visits were complete, the ride back to Harry's was quite long. The discussion of the day's visits was revealing as Cynthia led the discussion of what they had seen and heard.

Sarah was overwhelmed by the size of the empire her father had built. As she thought back over the visits, she was encouraged that the employees and supervisors all seemed to want to work there. It was a tribute to her father, and it made her even more determined to accept the responsibility of her position. She was so thankful that Terry was part of the decision. What would happen next was still unclear, but today was a good start.

"I would caution not to make significant changes until we can get the ownership documented and settled," Cynthia said.

"I agree," Rob said. "It will be a big enough challenge to take care of the legal transfer of ownership for now."

The discussion began to settle on a course of action, guided by Rob, the Casper attorneys, and Cynthia. There was an amazing wealth of suggestions and concerns that it be done the best possible way. Cynthia's husband was skillfully recording everything during their entire trip along with all the extra conversations so they could remember all that had taken place.

Tex and Jill had been quiet during most of the trip. Tex asked about the security detail at every plant, and Jill revealed she had interviewed some of the watchmen to see how they intended to keep the plant safe.

"Jill and I are also wondering if it wouldn't be advisable, especially with the uncertainties we are facing, to double or at least expand the protection at every plant," Tex said. "The supervisors could be pressured, even threatened, to take part in some shady or outright illegal activity and tempted to do so by promising to make it work to their benefit. They possibly already feel pressure from the new owner, even though our intention was to affirm them. We all felt anxious because of the experiences in Somewhere Valley when Sarah and those around her were threatened. It could happen again, and this change only adds to the uncertainty as well as the enormous financial value of the situation."

The silence on the bus was complete. No one had even considered this very real opportunity for evil to strike.

"I will see to that immediately," Cynthia said. "You are absolutely right in assuming it could be that some kind of scheme is already being planned. In fact, I will call my firm right now to employ a company we have worked with before to evaluate and harden the security at every plant for the workers on duty and consider more for decision makers. This is so timely. Thank you."

Rob began to sing, "Praise God from whom all blessings flow." Everyone joined in. Other songs were sung together in praise to

God and in asking for His protection and direction. The rest of the trip was truly a fitting end to a busy day.

It was nearly dark when the bus arrived at Harry's farm. The Fishers and Youngs went with their families for a night and day of needed renewal. The quiet evening around the firepit was refreshing after the tension-filled day. One by one people began to share how they had gotten to the place in their lives where they were today. Sarah hadn't shared anything, but she was drawn into the warmth of friends from Meeteetse and Somewhere Valley. Her thoughts went to the two girls they had left, and she wondered whether they had been able to grow in their lives and experiences.

The quiet sense of family was interrupted by the announcement of another person at the door asking for Janet and Jordan. Harry froze and looked at Janet. She was shaking, and he took her hand as they went toward the front door. Just before they could see who was there, Harry prayed that God would make this a confirmation of His grace and healing. Jordan opened the door, and his sister, Mary, smothered him. Janet wrapped her arms around them both, and they wept openly. Harry wiped tears from his eyes as he gently led them into an office beside the front door. The reunion was complete. The fears and anger were washed away, and God began to put the family back together. Harry was beside himself with joy. He took them to the backyard and loudly announced who had come to the cheers of all the Somewhere Valley folks.

Rob shared again how he and Lottie had become involved with Somewhere and met Terry at the bank. Lottie went to sit beside Sarah and whispered that she must tell her story. Sarah felt the fear creep around her again but knew it was right to do so.

As Sarah began to tell the story of her life as a girl in Ohio and the pain of being abducted, gasps were heard around the fire. Cynthia felt the tears flow, and most others were close to tears. As the terrors began to give way to the love of Jess and Molly, who had said very little during the whole trip, they took up the story of finding her in the Fishers' house and described the anguish of the months that followed.

Rob along with Sarah told the story of the trial and isolation. Jill talked about the strength and amazing trust in God Sarah had shown as she left her adopted home to go to the trial. Terry added his part of the story, discovering the broken-down house in the forest and realizing God had a plan for them if they just trusted Him to reveal it. He shared the events at their wedding and how much those experiences had made their love even deeper.

Sarah talked about the first night at the motel and the car alarm going off in the middle of the night. The many attempts to steal Sarah brought Tex back to Somewhere Valley and how he and Jill had now been more permanently assigned there.

Tex talked about his coming to truly follow Jesus and how Somewhere Valley had changed his whole outlook on life. The story drew every family in Somewhere Valley into remembering and realizing God's protection.

The Youngs shared about the days of hiding Sarah and Molly and the explosion that had demolished the Martins' home. The coming of Carrie and Rhonda and Ron and LaVerne's taking their first "Sally" helped them all to see God works, His miracle in their lives again and again. Lottie explained why they were called "Sally." The story went on for some time. The entire crew at Harry's farm and the Linderman clan felt tied to Somewhere Valley more than ever before. The day ended late in the evening with songs of praise and words of encouragement.

Sleep came slowly, but when it did, everyone slept the sleep of exhaustion. Thursday was a day of sightseeing. Harry had planned a few events and surprises that would introduce everyone to Ohio. Sarah decided she wanted to drive by the house she had grown up in. It was a bittersweet experience for everyone on the bus, and it helped to close a chapter of memories for Sarah.

Sheriff Parks's phone rang as they were headed back to the farm. As he talked, he became more and more excited and handed the phone to Sarah. The voices at the other end of the call said in unison, "Hi, Mom!" Sarah was overwhelmed and put the phone up to Terry's ear too. When Terry answered, the girls said, "Hi, Dad." The day ended with rejoicing as they listened to all that had been happening at the Hastings house and school.

"We want to thank you for a wonderful week," Mylon said as the call came to an end. "Having the girls here has been a real treat and an exciting adventure. Hope all has gone well there, and we are anxious to see you all again."

"It has been a good week," Terry said. "We have a lot to share when we get home, and we can hardly wait to get there. Bye for now."

When the call ended, everyone wanted to know what was going on. Sharing the events of the week brought gasps, laughter, and real thankfulness. Sheriff Parks and Lottie were anxious to get home and find out all the details of the girls' encounter and the outcome.

Someone mentioned the Fishers and the McNerneys. They didn't have long to wait to find out how their visits had been as they turned in at the farm about the same time as the bus. Harry insisted the families stay for the barbecue and get to know all the folks. The food, fellowship, and warmth of good friends were worth their late-night drive home.

Harry took Mary, Janet, Jordan, and Terry to a small office late that evening. "I want to ask you, Mary, if you would consider coming to the home ranch here in Ohio to work for me in the kitchen and do whatever else there is to do. You would have room and board as well as a salary. I need more help for the kitchen staff anyway. Would you consider being part of our family?"

"I haven't had a home for a long time," Mary said. "I never expected to ever be wanted by Mom, Jordan, or Terry again after all the trouble I have caused. You don't know me, but yes, I want to be part of a family again. I—I just don't know what to say."

"All you have to say is yes," Harry said. "I will have my foreman and kitchen staff make all the necessary arrangements for you. It would be a privilege for you to come to the farm."

The visit with Harry's foreman was all that was needed to seal the deal. He was so excited to have enough help in the kitchen, and he told Mary to come see him as soon as she could make arrangements at her current job.

Going home was on everyone's mind the next morning. Promises of visiting Somewhere Valley and the ready invitations were enjoyed all around. Suitcases and boxes of gifts and things to remember were loaded on the bus, and they headed for the airport. The Fisher and McNerney families were there to give them a great send-off and welcome them back anytime.

Harry was busy signing agreements for deals his construction company had landed in the last few days. It had definitely been a profitable trip for him too. The farm staff had come along to add their wishes and words of encouragement.

As the plane taxied and took off, turning west, Sarah melted into Terry's arms, and they enjoyed a special private conversation in the last seat on the plane.

"We will be home in just a few hours," Terry said. "I can't wait to hear about all the things the girls have experienced. It sounded like it was a regular Somewhere Valley week. One thing for sure, it sounds like they didn't lack for a lot excitement. I miss those rascals."

"Not any more than I do, I'm sure," Sarah said. "What will be next? Seeing all that we own was overwhelming. How can God use it for His glory and for the good of a lot of Sallys and more? What should we be doing with the resources that are available? Our board of directors, including all the folks in Somewhere Valley, will need to be wise counselors, but we have to be careful that the material stuff of all this isn't the most important thing in our lives. We need to decide just what we are going to try to do with all God has entrusted to us. I am so thankful for Cynthia. We couldn't have found a better representative. God has shown His goodness in His provision. We must use it wisely."

"I think Rob should be appointed as chairman of the board," Terry said. "He is wise about these things and can help point us in the right direction. Didn't he say once that he wanted to open an office in Meeteetse?" He softly added that having Mary in a safe place was a real blessing that couldn't be missed.

"His friend in Denver was who he wanted to be there," Sarah said. "I bet the Casper guys would be a help in this too. I really like them. They aren't pushy or know-it-all. Good choice, Rob. And I am so glad to meet Mary. Maybe she will be able to come to Somewhere Valley sometime."

Rob came back to talk to Terry and Sarah. He started going over the same things Terry and Sarah had just discussed. They laughed when they discovered they were already on the same page.

"So have you decided who is to be on the board?" Rob asked.

"We discussed it, and you are to be chairman," Sarah said. "You need to get your friend to Meeteetse as soon as possible. We can help them find land to build on, and I am sure there will be more work than they can do in a day."

"All the residents in Somewhere Valley should be on the board. New residents, probably not," Terry said. "We also really feel comfortable with Cynthia. She is very good at what she does and should probably be on the board too."

"It probably would be better not to have too many, but I think you are right. The Somewhere Valley ranchers should come first. Each one can decide if they want to participate. They would have to choose a chairman. Having Cynthia on the board might present a little problem with attending meetings, but with our new phone service, that issue also can be solved. I like your choices. What do you think of your girls' encounter?"

"Troubling to say the least. But as tough as Rhonda is, I can understand how they were able to pull it off. It is troubling that we still have some of the same problems. Maybe we need to hire a detective agency to really find out what is going on and if we can do anything about it," Sarah said.

"You're right. And it could be a real support to Sheriff Parks," Rob agreed. "Well, get some sleep. We should be home tonight, at least to Somewhere Valley. This has been a good trip, and the future doesn't seem nearly as cloudy it did."

With that the three friends tried to sleep in uncomfortable positions and were soon on the bus going toward Somewhere Valley.

CHAPTER 17

Sheriff Parks sighed as Meeteetse came into sight. "Home!" he said softly. No one had even thought of how much that word really meant until the bus turned off the highway and stopped at the General Store in Meeteetse. The familiar hills and forests were a welcome sight to the weary travelers, but not one person could think of any reason that it wasn't worth having gone. For Sarah, thoughts of home were her first priority. Somewhere Valley had become more important than ever before, and they were glad to be home. There was more mail than they had seen for a long time in their boxes at the General Store. Most of it was routine, but Jess Martin and Jim McNerney had a very official letter from the same place.

Jim and Leona were a little afraid to open their letter and find out what problem they had now.

When Jess opened his letter, he let out a whoop that might have been heard in Ohio.

"What is wrong?" Molly said. "How bad is it?"

"Listen to this everyone!" Jess said. As he read aloud, he came to the paragraph that said, "'Our firm wants to negotiate with you for the rights to mine the precious minerals on your ranch. We are prepared to pay top dollar to begin operation as soon as possible. In addition, we wish to protect your grass and pasture for your livestock. Please contact us as soon as possible.'"

Jim McNerney had just come to that same paragraph and turned to Leona and said, "Well, looks like you are going to get you a log house after all. I can't believe this is happening to us. I don't know about the rest of you, but we have been blessed beyond all imagination. Just to see our children and restore some kind of bond is more than worth the trip. So Harry, with all our hearts, we want to thank you for all your hospitality and provision. We couldn't have done it without you, and I am sure God never intended to do it without you either."

The remaining miles home were filled with singing and praising God for all He had done.

AUTHOR'S NOTE

If you began the journey in Somewhere Valley, Wyoming, at the beginning of this book, a lot of the story may have seemed somewhat strange. Knowing the people and places in the beginning will take you on a journey of success and failure.

Writing a story is wonderful. You can make it come out just like you want it to. All the fears and trials of life are less scary because you can shape the outcome. Going through the journey with Terry and Sarah has been an experience of its own. I have lived the fear, encountered the intruders, and felt the joy of success, the pain of disappointment, and the love they had for each other. I shed tears as they struggled, and as they triumphed, I rejoiced. It has been a great journey from "lost" to "settled," but I hope it serves only to point each of us toward the One who really can solve life's most difficult problems.

We can't make the future what we want it to be in real life. We must anticipate life in the light of God's care and compassion for us as we go along. The future of the characters in Somewhere Valley could be just like you or me. They didn't know what was coming toward them either. In fact, the author didn't always know how everything was going to turn out, so the story was written for them just as our story is for us.

God knows the outcome of our story, and He knows how to get there even when we don't. It is our responsibility to put our trust in Him so when the story of our lives, uncertain as it may be, comes to the final chapter, we will be confident that the end will be where God wants us to be.

Blessings on you, reader. May you find the source of confidence in God's plan so compelling that your life will be lived for His best, even if it doesn't appear to be working out very well.

Printed in the United States
by Baker & Taylor Publisher Services